Contents

FLAME
Angels

An Anthology of Irish Writing

edited by Polly Nolan

Mammoth

For my parents, with love and thanks.
PN

First published in Great Britain in 2000 by Mammoth
an imprint of Egmont Children's Books Limited,
239 Kensington High Street, London W8 6SA

ISBN 0 7497 3958 4

10 9 8 7 6 5 4 3 2 1

A CIP catalogue record for this title is available from the British Library

Typeset by M Rules
Printed in Great Britain
by Cox & Wyman Ltd, Reading, Berkshire

Contents

Flower Child

June Considine

Across the road from the bookshop, the Liffey flowed on an incoming tide. The water rose so slowly it was hard to know that anything was changing until it crept above the dank brown steps. Then Ally could no longer smell the rubbish on the river bed and there was a freshness in the air she had learned to recognise. Seagulls swooped low over the wall, their eyes glittering, searching for food. She remembered the way they used to descend on her granny's garden, flocks of them, screeching as they chased the smaller birds, ripping plastic bags of rubbish with their sharp angry beaks and strutting along the window ledge.

'Dirty scavengers!' Her granny always shouted, rapping hard on the kitchen window to chase them away. Scavengers, living just to eat someone else's leftovers.

Last night Ally ate a hamburger that had been dumped in a litter bin. It was still warm, but hard, as if it had been fried in too much grease and, even now, to think about it made her stomach queasy. At Ricky's Diner the chef was her friend. His name was Jack and he sounded like Daniel O'Donnell, soft and easy when he spoke. At the back of the restaurant so much food was dumped from plates she never could get used to it. Steaks and chicken legs and spare ribs with lots of meat still on the bone. Sometimes, when the manager went home early, Jack brought her into the kitchen and gave her food with no one else's teeth marks on it. He said she was a walking disaster waiting to happen. A daft wee thing, as daft as she was pretty, which was probably a nice thing to hear, but she wasn't sure about anything any more. Last week she had told him about the house in the country and he had said, 'Wake up, Ally child, and smell the coffee. There's no house.'

'Yes, there is.' It was important that he believe her. 'Lots of holiday houses. Clara says no one bothers with them except in the summer time.'

'And you think you'll be able to stay in one of them?' He forced her to look at him. 'That no one will see you and run your little ass out of there so fast you won't see the mountain for dust. I know about such places. Even the stone walls have eyes.'

'No one sees me here and there's millions of people about,' she replied, angry that he was making fun of her. She didn't tell him about the night of the Telethon when everyone was raising money for charity, and how, since then, she'd known that her old life had not really gone away but could suddenly appear, tapping without warning at her elbow.

He wrapped chicken in tinfoil for her to take back to Clara. 'Don't pay a blind bit of notice to that old biddy,' he warned. 'She stopped living in the real world centuries ago. The only house she has is tucked inside her mind.'

Outside the bookshop a barrow holding the second-hand books had a canopy protecting them from the sun and high red wheels. The first book she opened smelled musty. It had yellow, brittle pages, a broken spine and tea stains on the cover as if someone had used it for a saucer. All the cardinal sins, she thought, listing them the way her English teacher, Miss McCarthy, used to do. Don't make dog ears. Don't bend back the spine. Never put your cup down on a book, which is a precious thing and must be respected.

When Miss McCarthy talked about books she gave them personalities, as if they were real people. Some were uplifting, she said, and thought-provoking. Some were full of negative energy that made you depressed or angry without understanding why. Some were good bed companions. When you couldn't sleep in the small hours of the morning it was a pleasure to hold a good blockbuster in your hands. The class howled when she came out with that one and Miss McCarthy laughed too, blushing, knowing she'd walked right into it. The pupils in First Year D laughed a lot during English class. They said Miss McCarthy was off the wall, wired to the moon, but they laughed with her and not at her.

Ally was surprised at how easily the memory came back. As if it was stored somewhere dark and safe until the right moment came to set it free. She couldn't remember when she'd last read a book or even held one in her hands. After her granny died she read so much she never seemed to have time for anything else. No time to think about what she'd lost, Granny and the house on Barry Parade where the two of them had lived together for fourteen years. Rose, her real mother, would get annoyed when she found her reading, even though Ally stayed quiet in the deepest corner of the sofa. She said Ally was copping out and she'd be better occupied smiling occasionally and making herself useful round the place. The house on Barry Road had been sold so that Rose would have enough money to look after her. Ally found it hard to remember what it looked like. When she went back once to see it, the new people had made changes, stained glass windows in the hall door, a rockery in the front garden, a dog that growled through the bars of the gate.

The man inside the bookshop kept staring at her. After a while he came out, pretending to look through the second-hand books. 'Can I help you, Miss?' he asked. He had black curly hair and tiny glasses perched on his nose which gave him a snooty expression.

'Just looking,' she said, turning away from him.

'I'm just looking too,' he warned, going back inside to serve a customer. He had called his shop Wordy Cause which, as far as Ally was concerned, said enough about his particular personality.

She placed the musty book back on the barrow and began to search for one about flowers. 'Knowledge is power,' Miss McCarthy used to say. When Ally moved to the house in the country with Clara she would want to know the names of all the wild flowers that grew along the lanes and in the hedgerows. Nothing was real unless it had a name. Her granny named her after a flower. Alyssum, after the little white plants that grew in rock gardens. People always thought her name was Alison. Not that it mattered really. For as long as she could remember she had been called Ally by everyone except Miss McCarthy, who believed a person's name was an essential part of their identity and should never be abbreviated.

At last she found the book she wanted. Heavy and thick, full of knowledge. Paintings of flowers, each one with a name and a description. The man in the bookshop watched her, waiting to see what she would do. She began to read, whispering the words to herself. *Wood Anemone:* deep-cut leaves, long stalks, grows in drifts on the edge of woods, poisonous. *Irish Spurge:* medium-sized perennial, yellow-green leafy group, grows prolifically in Kerry, poisonous. How strange. She had never thought of flowers as poisonous. They grew wild in the house where she lived with Clara. From cracks in the walls and ceilings, green banks of flowers with white heads like trumpets. Fragile pink flowers shaped like stars, rooting in the concrete floor. She had watched them spread, stretching greedy suckers into the air, demanding space to survive. She supposed they were really weeds but it still amazed her that anything could grow in the crumbling debris.

When Ally ran away, Clara took care of her. They met under a bridge when Ally tripped over her in the darkness. At first, in her confusion, she thought Clara was a mummy, one of those Egyptian ones wrapped in sheets, but the sheets came alive and a raspy voice ordered her to have a bit of respect for other people's privacy. If she wanted to lie down and be quiet there was a blanket to spare. It smelled musty and felt damp but after a while she grew warm and in the morning Clara shared peaches from a tin can with her.

Clara knew everything about the streets. She was like a fierce watchdog, barking at men if they stared too long at Ally or made suggestions. They called Clara a wino and an alcho but, more often, they just said she was a crazy old bag, especially when she started shouting, her grey witchy hair falling to her shoulders. Ally's granny never believed in grey hairs. Once a month she dyed her hair with Red Hot Sizzle. Ally had to check the roots carefully so that not a single strand escaped. She had an old face, puckered like an accordion but, until the day she died, her hair was the colour of ripe raspberries.

On the first Saturday of every month they used to visit Rose, who lived in a terraced house with Sam and their five children. They were Ally's half-sisters and brothers, younger than her, and always staring as if she was an unwelcome stranger. Rose was usually ironing or cooking when they arrived. She never seemed to remember they were coming or thank them for the *Teatime Express* cakes they brought with them.

'You could have rung to remind me,' she'd say, looking cross. 'I'm up to my eyes with the kids.'

When Sam was around she was jittery, so tense they never stayed for long. He stared at Ally from hard, button eyes. He pinched her arm when no one was looking and pulled her close to him. He said she was pampered, a prize doll, full of herself. When he went out to meet his friends in the pub Rose hugged Ally as if she was really sorry to see her go. Her granny said Sam was the jealous type who couldn't stand the thought of Rose loving someone else before she married him. Ally hoped her real father had been nicer than Sam.

'Oh, he was a proper dream boat, all right.' Her granny used to roll her eyes in admiration whenever she talked about him. His name was Patrick and she taught him to jive to her collection of Buddy Holly records. It used to embarrass Rose to see her mother acting like a young one with no sense at all, but Patrick thought she was a real raver with her Red Hot Sizzle hair and fancy feet. He jived out of their lives after he had promised to marry Rose. Granny believed he jived all the way to Australia and was probably still jiving there now with the kangaroos. When Ally asked her mother what he was *really* like, Rose snapped, 'Ask no questions and you'll be told no lies.'

After Patrick left she gave her wedding dress to an Oxfam shop. She gave Ally to her mother when she was born five months later. A wonderful gift, said Granny, one that could never be taken back. Ally was glad she didn't live in a house that smelled of babies and boiled-over milk and a man who barked, 'Salt!' if it wasn't sitting under his nose on the table.

When her granny died, Ally had to move in there. At night she slept with her half-sisters, four of them together in the one bedroom. They giggled and talked about her under the duvets. Sam said there wasn't money for an extra mouth and that Ally's granny was a miserable old skinflint who left nothing but expense behind her. Ally said he was a liar. What about the money from Granny's house? He said he'd take his fist to her lip if she didn't put a zip on it. Instead, he hit Rose. Suddenly one night, without warning. Rose looked small, as if she'd shrunk into an old woman's body. Ally wanted to run between them. She wanted to hit him back, the same hard smack of flesh on bone, but her mother shouted at her to go upstairs. She'd caused enough trouble since she arrived.

After Ally ran away she became clever at spotting people she knew and fading out from the crowd before they noticed her. 'A slippery fish,' Clara called her. 'Slipping right through the net.' The house where they lived had once been a warehouse used for storing cargo when the ships sailed up the river to be unloaded by dockers. The dockers had gone and the ships had cargo that rolled on and off. Soon the warehouse would disappear. Apartments would rise in its place and the flowers would die, rootless under metal girders and marble floors.

Some nights when she waited for Clara to come back,

Ally imagined how different it would be in the country. When she grew frightened and there was still no sign of Clara she repeated the names of the flowers she knew, whispering them over and over again until her eyelids felt heavy: violets, cowslips, bluebells, primroses, buttercups, foxgloves, daisies, forget-me-nots. On the other side of the Liffey, the windows of high empty office blocks quivered with reflections and the city lights danced in the green glass.

Flowers were drugs, Clara said. Animals in the jungles and the rainforests were forever stoned out of their heads. She was always throwing out bits of information. Even though she couldn't name the stoned animals or the drug-plants it was nice at night to sit and listen to her, especially when they lit a fire and the wood spat and crackled and sparks fluttered in the darkness like luminous moths. Then Clara sang Joni Mitchell songs in a voice so husky she had to screech the high notes. The fire killed the flowers. In the morning there would be a black burned patch on the ground and the leaves near the heat were shrivelled, like old blistered skin.

Clara talked a lot about the Sixties. 'Make love. Not war.' She'd had flowers in her hair and a kaftan with purple embroidery. She went to America and marched in protests demanding civil rights for black people and an end to Vietnam and famine and bombs and everything else that was wrong in the world.

'We really made a difference,' she said, proudly. 'We made it all happen.'

When Clara was a child she lived in *Slí na hAbhann*. The way of the river she said, because outside her gate a river splashed over rocks, leaping and falling and disappearing into mossy crevices and ditches of white thorned bushes. It sounded lovely to Ally but Clara shook her head until her witchy hair fell over her face. *Slí na hAbhann* was a black hole on the edge of a Kerry mountain, dead on its feet except for a few months in the tourist season. Then the people from the city came, opening up their holiday homes, drinking pints of mountain air, spaced out on turf smoke and heather and the roar of the river making waterfalls. Soon the houses were empty again and the only things moving on the horizon were sheep with black faces and an odd mountain goat. Clara's breath wheezed when she spoke too fast. She moaned in her sleep, her body shaking and twitching. If she wet herself it did not embarrass her because she never realised what she had done and Ally had learned to stop thinking about it.

Until the night of the Telethon Ally believed she was an invisible part of the city. What a mad crazy night it had been, people in fancy dress singing in groups, marching in bands and walking high on stilts. They looked so happy because it was the one night of the year that everyone came together to raise money for charity and go on television waving enormous cheques. The people did not notice her outstretched hand. She stood on the edge of the pavement as they flowed past on a wave of noise and laughter. They rattled their collection boxes, bullying everyone into giving money and she was alone in the crowded street until Miss McCarthy touched her arm.

'Alyssum, how are you?' she asked, her eyes startled. 'I've been worried sick about you.' Instead of a pile of English copy-books she carried a guitar. In jeans and a white T-shirt with the Telethon logo she looked so young. She moved closer. Ally was ready to run but the teacher's voice stayed her, as if she was back again in First Year D in the third row, being ordered to pay attention. Living rough only meant moving in one direction, Miss McCarthy said. The downward graph. It solved nothing. Time to go home.

'I've no home,' Ally was fierce and determined. 'Not since Granny died. I can't go back to them . . . I won't!'

Miss McCarthy looked as if she was going to cry. 'There are people who can help you make a new home. Just trust me.' She wrote her phone number on a piece of paper, big bold numbers, and handed it to Ally. 'Think about what I've said and ring me. Please . . . please trust me.'

Clara broke them apart, shouting. 'The lunatics have escaped from the asylum! Let's get the hell out of here!' She pointed towards a group of men dressed as women, glitzy pink hair, big boobs with spangles that flashed as they danced *Riverdance* on a pavement in the middle of O'Connell Street where the flower-sellers sat in the daytime selling carnations. When the men stopped kicking their legs and opened hip flasks, she came back and said, 'Have you a drop of the hard stuff to spare, lads?'

They turned away, embarrassed when they saw her. Her laughter had a wild pitch that frightened Ally. It wasn't a safe sound and she knew she could do nothing to make it different.

Miss McCarthy was still talking when Ally ran. Afterwards she found the paper with the telephone number in her pocket. She was going to throw it away but Clara was acting so weird she forgot. Usually, when Clara spoke about *Slí na hAbhann*, her voice rasped with anger. Ally would wonder why she kept saying she wanted to go back to live there. That night her voice was calm. She talked about the country lanes in the morning after the rain stopped falling. Ladybirds on the stems of flowers. Hammocks of fine silver thread swaying from blades of grass. Hedgerows hanging heavy with bells of fuchsia and the dizzy scent of heather on the breeze. On such a morning the world was a prayer, she said. You stood still and became one with the air and the sunshine and the great white energy of the mountain. In the city you couldn't smell flowers because there was no stillness, only constant motion.

13

* * *

Last night Clara lay on the ground and began to rock. She gathered her knees into her chest and rocked on her back, forwards and backwards. Her face was slack, her lips moist and blue. It was horrible to watch but Ally didn't know how to stop her. When she lay still her eyes were flat, as if someone had switched off a light inside her. Ally ran and dialled 999 and men came with a stretcher, clambering over the broken walls and glass, and lifted her gently off the ground. Ally stayed in the shadows, invisible, and when the siren faded she took the bus to the hospital with the high curved steps and wondered which window Clara lay behind.

The man in the bookshop had stopped watching her. Quickly, she shoved the flower book under her anorak and sprinted away, dodging traffic and running over the Halfpenny Bridge, the sound of her footsteps drumming in her ears, almost as loud as her heartbeat. In Temple Bar she smelled coffee and garlic. She recognised the boys who sometimes slept in the warehouse. She could no longer think of it as a house since Clara was taken away. The boys had sharp faces and, like the seagulls, eyes that only noticed what was necessary for their survival. They knew about Clara and the hospital. She'd had blood tests and spent the night screeching abuse at the nurses. It always amazed Ally how word on the street spread. As if jungle drums were beating out the news under the layers of the city. She ran on, not stopping until she reached the warehouse.

Builders in yellow hats and jackets had arrived. They stuck tripods into the ground and their thick wellingtons trampled the flowers. Their eyes slid over Ally as if she was not there. One of them kicked aside an empty wine bottle. 'Go home, kid,' he said. 'This place is coming down soon and the sooner the better.'

Along the Liffey bank she walked, down the quays where the walls were bright with graffiti, past the ships with foreign flags and the cranes that lit the skyline at night. The flower book was heavy in her arms. A man walked out in front of the traffic, ignoring the angry drivers who blasted their horns and shouted. He lifted a traffic cone and dropped it into the water. He just raised it above his head and let it fall, not even looking over the wall to see the splash. From the expression on his face as he shambled past she knew he had stopped thinking long ago. She had seen him with Clara a few times, the two of them sitting on steps, not talking, just looking straight ahead, sharing a bottle.

She came to a bench and sat down, suddenly so tired she did not think she would ever again have the energy to move. She opened the book and stared at the pictures. So many flowers. She would never remember the names. The tears came suddenly, streaking her cheeks, surprising her they fell so fast. Her eyes were gritty when she tried to wipe them away. She thought about the mountain and the houses and the empty spaces just waiting to be filled. She smelled the river and the yeast from the brewery and the smell of Clara, the flower child, who had decided a long time ago that her mind was the only safe place to live. She would be out of hospital soon. Only the warehouse would be gone. And she would return to *Slí na hAbhann* only in her dreams.

The crumpled piece of paper with Miss McCarthy's bold handwriting was still in the pocket of her anorak. She allowed her fingers to rest on it for a moment then began to walk away, slowly at first, until she saw the telephone kiosk and her footsteps quickened as she imagined the strong voice of her teacher leading her safely home. Above her the clouds formed a daisy chain, casting shapes on the Liffey, streaks of violet, the bluebell sky and the sun, as yellow as a buttercup, touching her hair.

Coming Home

Dermot Bolger

Shane Brennan placed his bag down on the vast green opposite his house where the horses were tethered. They shied away as if from a stranger – although, of all the lads along the Crescent, he'd always had a gift with animals. He tried approaching Joey McCormack's old black horse tethered to a rope. It shied away, then let Shane run his fingers through its tangled mane. But the youth couldn't be sure if this was because the horse still remembered him or was so broken in health and spirit as to be beyond caring.

Maybe there was a time when horses hadn't grazed here, ridden in and out of Smithfield market to be bought and sold by boys. But Shane's earliest memories were of waking to a distant whinnying and padding across to stare from his bedroom window at those great patient beasts standing sentinel-like on the moonlit grass.

That's what he'd missed most during the last three years living in digs in England. He'd missed his family and pals, of course, but everybody who signed schoolboy forms at the football club missed those. The horses were different and he had found he couldn't properly talk about them – not even to the other boys, until Farrell O'Riordan came. Homesickness was a symptom the club understood. They even had pep talks about it from their coach, a former Scottish international who'd broken his leg playing for the reserves while trying to come back from a series of cartilage operations. But the Brits simply wouldn't have it in them to want to understand about the horses, except for maybe one or two of the black lads.

At least he was here on his own two feet, unlike Farrell. Maybe now Shane would finally phone him, like he'd been promising himself for weeks.

The green sloped slightly towards the church, before falling away down a steep hill. A thousand times he had chased a football down it, deftly controlling it with a flick to prevent the ball bouncing into the passing traffic. He had always been the youngest on any team, sent to do the fetching and carrying, and yet still picked first. By the age of nine he was sick of playing kids his own size. Four years, five years older, he didn't care. The bigger they came the easier they were to nutmeg. They shied away from kicking him until ten minutes into the game when they would forget his age, or remember it and get angry.

Playing on that waterlogged green had prepared him for any rough treatment he ever received togging out for Tolka Rangers in the Dublin Schoolboy League. At least in league games there was a referee. By the age of eleven he had been aware of arguments at the club about what age group he should play for. The Under 12s would win the league without him. The Under 13s desperately needed a striker. Not that Eddie, the Under 12s manager, ever gave way. Shane was his star and Shane trusted him, even though Eddie would give Shane as much of a barracking as any other player who stepped out of line.

They all came to watch that year when the Under 12s went unbeaten in the league and two cups. Scouts from Arsenal, Liverpool, Spurs, Celtic and even clubs like Brighton, Blackpool and Tranmere whom nobody even knew had scouts in Ireland. 'You can look but you cannot touch,' Eddie would mutter, and look they certainly did. Not just at Shane but at Derek in midfield and Eamo in goals.

If Eddie made sure they didn't touch then Eddie wasn't always around. The knocks on the door generally came at the same time – five minutes past eight approximately. Maybe the clubs presumed that players' mothers watched *Coronation Street* and there were rules about getting into their bad books by disturbing them. After these three years nothing would surprise him about the tricks and strategies that clubs used.

They always arrived quietly. Friendly middle-aged men with weatherworn faces in unobtrusive cars, who wanted nothing stronger than a cup of tea and a quiet word. He didn't want them to be quiet. Back then he'd wanted to open his bedroom window and tell the whole Crescent that the representative from some Premiership team was sitting in his kitchen. Parts of the conversations he was allowed to sit in on, but for other parts he was sent upstairs. His age was the big stumbling block back then, being too young to sign for anyone. But his fourteenth birthday was approaching. Everything could change if his parents would stop listening to Eddie and give him his chance to go.

Not that he was always sure he wanted to go. Eddie had gone, back in the 1970s, though he didn't talk of it much. It was hard to think of that man who sold gas cylinders from an open-backed truck ever being photographed by the *Evening Herald* about to board an aeroplane. Shane's da didn't want him to go, but Shane knew he wouldn't stand in his way. All his life Da had been like a shadow on the touchline, never interfering but always there, never allowing him to get too thrilled about a hat-trick or too downhearted over losing.

His ma was the stumbling block. The closer his birthday came, the more it gnawed at her. Was she standing in his way, holding him back because he was her first born? But why did they want him so young? She'd keep asking. Why couldn't he finish his education first and have something to fall back on? Once or twice when Da was at work and Marie and Sam were playing upstairs, she'd look at him and start crying, and he would cry too, both of them at the kitchen table not knowing what to do.

And then *the* club came knocking, like a summons nobody could ignore. All his life his dream hadn't been to play for them but simply to be allowed to see a match in their ground. His bedroom wall was covered in their posters. He had sat in the kitchen, knowing this was it, and when he'd looked across at his mother he'd known that she knew it too. Her resistance was broken. Not even Eddie's arguments worked, and Shane had hated him that evening he called over. Shane was one step from paradise, with this raggle-taggle has-been trying to keep him a little boy for ever. 'Just because you were a bloody failure doesn't mean I'll be one too!' he'd suddenly screamed at the man. There had been no way to take the words back. Eddie had left soon afterwards. Shane always planned to make it up, by stating in interviews how much the man had done for him. But no interviews ever came.

He knew that he shouldn't have boarded a cheap coach by himself last night. He should at least have told his family he was coming, but that would have been worse. They would have insisted he fly and been waiting at the airport, not knowing what to say. Nobody in his family would say a word against him, but he knew he'd failed himself and failed them. It would come out in whispers, in Sam being taunted at school and, if Shane ever bothered playing on that green again, in tackles that people would never have dared attempt a year before when he had arrived home with Farrell O'Riordan as somebody still to be reckoned with.

He remembered that weekend of his sixteenth birthday. Farrell and he sat like kings on the garden wall surrounded by girls. Farrell wasn't even somebody he would have palled around with in Ireland. They would never have met, except as rival fans at Shelbourne versus Cork City matches. Farrell was built like a hardman and acted like one too, whereas Shane was slight and swift and always being told to stay behind and work on the weights. But they were both Irish and that was enough for the club to pair them off when Farrell arrived, switching their digs so that they shared, and letting them sink or swim together.

No one knew the difference between Cork and Dublin

in England anyway. They had the same jibes and sly digs to cope with and yet people liked the fact that they were Irish. It made them seem novel, different, expected to be the life and soul of parties, to sing and tell jokes at the drop of a hat. And Farrell could. Not just pop songs, but ancient *come-all-yizs* from Cork, about drink and women, that nobody had heard before and that even the driver on the team bus would stop talking to listen to.

The pros tolerated Farrell too, especially the continental ones who loved when he stood on the training pitch sideline to give running commentaries, mispronouncing their names in a mock BBC accent, before being chased off. Nobody else dared do it, but nobody else would get away with it. It was the Cork charm laid on in thick doses when necessary. Farrell could have talked his way out of anything except that sliding tackle two minutes into injury time in a meaningless game in an empty stadium in France.

The trip was just a perk to kick-start their final season together, before apprentice contracts were offered to a chosen few. They were soft games against French kids who might have been playing in snowshoes for all the talent they had.

When Farrell got the ball he didn't even look around. They were seven goals up. God knows why the ref. was playing injury time. Farrell should have laid it off first time but took too long, drawing the moment out for effect like he sometimes stretched a punchline. He never even saw the tackle coming from behind, but really it wasn't a tackle, more an assault.

There was no video camera recording the moment, but Shane didn't need reminders. Every night for the next month he saw it happen slowly in his mind, the studs thudding against the knee bone, the leg contorting out of shape and that snap – a sound like no other – before the bone protruded and blood came. Farrell had started screaming but Shane didn't really hear him. It was as if that snap had silenced everything else as it reverberated inside his skull. There was a fight that became a free-for-all with even trainers involved. The kid who'd fouled him was a puny nobody who had just been told by the club that he was being let go. The French players gathered round him, defending him with football's mob mentality, even though Shane could see that they wanted to kill him too. Then suddenly the pitch was cleared, with players bustled back onto the bus and told their clothes would be brought by car to the hotel, while Farrell lay, screaming on the grass, being attended to by two men.

They had to operate twice. 'Stuff this for a game of cowboys,' Farrell joked when Shane visited him in hospital. 'When they kept talking about trying to put some metal into us, I didn't think they meant three screws in my leg.'

Nobody could say that the club didn't do enough for

him. The best of doctors, then they flew him back to Cork first class. Anyone can break their leg at any time, but Shane had always imagined it at Anfield or Highbury with the crowd rising to you and cameras and lights. Now he knew it could happen at any moment, any tackle, even a meaningless training session on a wet Tuesday afternoon. It affected them all in the following weeks, so that the coach had to keep screaming, 'Are you men or poofs?' *Poof* was one of his favourite words, making him seem like a ludicrous Brylcreemed figure from the Middle Ages. But football was full of such brainless prejudice, people afraid to speak their minds on anything that wasn't in the tabloids, frightened of the ridicule of the herd. The coach had obviously been proving he was no 'poof' when he broke his own leg and lost his house and model wife with it. Gradually the other lads forgot their fear. But they weren't returning to digs with an empty room across the corridor and to Mrs Allen who had broken down in tears the night that Farrell left.

'The loveliest lad,' she'd said, 'but I always knew he was wasting his time here. I've almost stopped taking in his type.'

'What type?' Shane had asked and Mrs Allen stopped, as if realising what she had said.

'You Irish,' Mr Allen replied quietly beside her. 'I know there's a history of Irish pros playing for the club, but they've always been bought in from other clubs. I mean, I've seen dozens of you up and down the stairs here, but it's forty years since any Irish lad has made it from apprentice to the first team. And sure with all the money at stake now, who's going to take a chance on you anyway unless you're God Almighty? The stakes are too high. If any gap appears at all, they go across to Europe with a cheque book and buy experience.'

Shane stepped off the grass and crossed towards the first terrace of houses on the Crescent. Nobody was about yet, but some kid in pyjamas appeared in the window of McCormacks' house to stare down. It must be Joey's brother who'd only been a baby when Shane left. Ever since he was five Shane had called for Joey McCormack to walk to school together. Inseparable, kicking football for hours against his garden wall. The first summer he was home Joey had been all over him, wanting to know about the dressing-rooms and grounds and training schedules. But more recently he'd become distant, until he almost appeared puzzled by why Shane was calling. It was jealousy, Shane had thought at first, but now he knew it wasn't. It was indifference. Joey had moved on, with new friends, new interests, a new life. All his old pals had. The team broke up with the better ones playing for Cherry Orchard and Home Farm. Eddie had started from scratch again, giving his heart and soul to a bunch of snot-nosed eight-year-olds.

With Eddie you always knew where you stood. In England you learned to mull over every remark. Anything of importance was said out of earshot, behind your back. In these last months when people came to look at him again it was different from being twelve and under Eddie's wing. Now they stood on the edge of pitches, high-up faces stopping by unannounced to watch the second half of games. All the lads knew this time it was for real: this wasn't a selection, it was a culling. Merciless, calculating eyes that left nowhere to hide. The mood among the lads was different now, with a sudden edge, knowing that only a few would survive the cut.

Before that trip to France Shane had never doubted that he would be one of those offered contracts, and Farrell too. Maybe one or two other players had more skill but they were headless chickens, not so much without discipline as without brains. He had overcome homesickness so bad that some nights he'd had his bags packed for a cheap coach to Ireland. He had put on weight, shown enough character and coolness to be allowed to wear the captain's armband on occasions. But now, when it mattered, Shane found himself chickening out of challenges. Not blatantly so that an ordinary spectator would see, but holding back enough for watching eyes on the touchline to notice and for other players to sense his fear and exploit it.

Nobody had questioned his courage before. He had

stitches above his eye and had broken a rib in his first year. But every night he woke in a sweat, hearing that same snap of bone and the sickening silence before Farrell's scream. No Irish player had made it in the club in forty years, so why the hell did they keep coming? He could be sitting his Leaving Certificate exam in Dublin, walking to school with Joey, eyeing up girls, maybe playing National League B with his da watching from the empty stands.

Instead he was out of sight, out of mind. Once he had made it to the Irish Under 16 panel. His mother phoned, saying a neighbour had seen it on the Teletext. There was a call to the club, then somebody on the books of Huddersfield Town recovered from injury and regained his place. Huddersfield Town. The Irish team had gone on to win the Under 16 European Championship, with the final shown live on Irish television. They came home as heroes like Jack Charlton's teams, crowds at the airport, an open topped bus and everything. Half of them were signed to Mickey Mouse teams in the lower divisions or back in Ireland. His mother had sent him the press cuttings. Da would have known never to do that.

He was home now and would never go back to that stadium, even as a spectator. That famous football club which worked like a coffee grinder. You were a player, you had your pass. You walked along plush carpets, ate the best food and yet you were nobody. A face in the corridor that nobody really noticed was gone after you got called into the manager's room. He'd seen it too often already, lads of seventeen and eighteen sitting alone in the empty stand, crying their eyes out. How people avoided them till they were gone and how there was always some starry-eyed fourteen-year-old with his parents being shown round.

During the last four games of the season he lost it altogether, like his body was filled with lead, exhausted after ten minutes, so frantic to make up lost ground that he couldn't pace himself properly. Each time he was substituted, sitting apart from the others on the bench, noticing how the coach stopped offering encouragement or advice. Every game got worse and where once the lads would have slagged him now they said nothing. It was the instincts of the pack. With him and Farrell gone, there might be a chance of an extra year's contract for another one of them.

He wasn't just coming home this morning, he was running away. He told himself that at least he was doing it in his own way, saving himself from that indignity of being called into the office, which almost the entire team would endure over the next few days. Two at most would make it to next season, although they all believed it was going to be them because they were afraid to face the emptiness once they walked out through that door. He was facing it here in his own way, taking back control of his life.

He didn't know if he'd bother playing again. Because even if he managed to join Shelbourne, as Eddie had suggested years ago, he would never be known as the kid who was good enough to play for them. Instead he would be the kid who was only good enough to play for Shelbourne. The kid who got sent home from England, the boy with the golden touch and the brilliant future already behind him.

He stopped at his gate. There seemed to be nobody up yet or at least no light in the hall. His da's old Sunny was parked in the narrow driveway he'd built in the garden. A burst football lay there that Sam must have been kicking around. There seemed no way past the wooden door into the side passageway, but if you reached your hand over you could open the bolt on the far side.

The dog came down by the side of the house to greet him, not bounding but slowly, his leg stiffened by arthritis. At least he didn't bark as if at an intruder. Shane dropped his bag and knelt to put his arms round the dog. His coat smelled and so did his breath, but his eyes had that same look, as though slightly puzzled by life.

Once Shane stood up he knew that he would have to face them all – Da, Ma, Sam, Marie – face that cramped kitchen which seemed to get smaller with every visit home. Face the bedroom he would now share with the kid brother who didn't really know him after three years away. He patted the dog once more and rose. There was a pale light in the kitchen. He knew his da would be up before any of the family, starting the breakfasts, ready to call up the stairs.

His da turned as Shane opened the kitchen door. He was frying bacon. He eyed the travel bag.

'It's yourself,' was all he said. 'The hard man. Would you go a rasher?'

Only twice in his life had Shane seen his da lose his temper. That unflappable quality, and the way you never quite knew what he was thinking, used to annoy Shane. Even when Shane signed for the club he had refused to get overexcited. But now he was thankful for the lack of questioning, for the way Da was buying time for him.

'I wouldn't mind one,' he said. 'I'm starving.'

He sat at the table. Not even the mugs had changed in three years. He'd missed this house so much, yet now it didn't seem like his home. How would he ever fit back here? His father was cooking away, making as little noise as possible.

'I got sent home,' Shane said. 'They don't think I've got the bottle. They're not going to offer me a contract.'

'They should have phoned,' his da said. 'It shouldn't be you having to tell me.'

'It's not official till Friday. I just didn't want to wait around, have people looking at me. It's hard enough without the whole world knowing that you've failed.'

'Failed?' Shane saw that his da's hand was shaking as he put the rasher and black pudding on a plate. The man turned. His eyes were clear and blue, staring directly at him. 'Son, you haven't even started yet.'

Freak

Michael Tubridy

'Austin, you're a bleedin' freak, you are,' Darren says in class one day in first year when Mr Carew is handing back history tests. Austin has scored one hundred per cent again.

'The right sort of freak, Darren?' asks Mr Carew.

'I dunno, sir, I just know my ma'd freak if she knew I got seventeen per cent.'

'Have you heard of parent-teacher meetings, Darren? There's one next week . . .'

'Ah, sewer! Coulden ya mix up my marks with Austin's? I wouldn't mind bein' a freak just for one day . . .'

'I'm not sure I like you calling Austin a freak . . .'

'Sir, he is! He's a geek too, aren't ya, Brainbox? But I love him!' He leans over me and gives Austin a bearhug and a pretend slobbery kiss.

Austin is grinning fit to burst and looking geekier than ever, just like a swot from the *Beano* with his wispy hair and granddad glasses. He grabs Darren round the neck. 'Aw, Darren, diddums! Give Austy-wausty a big cuddly-wuddly!'

'Ah, me neck!' squawks Darren, pulling away. 'Get off, ya mad little squirt!'

The whole class is cracking up, Mr Carew too, not that I can see too well with Darren's elbow jammed into my gullet.

Looking back now from the dossy depths of transition year, first year was really good and it was mainly thanks to Mr Carew who was our form teacher and taught us both English and history.

'Lads!' he always called us, or 'Leds' as he pronounced it. 'Down to business, leds!'

It was incredible how much work we did. The Greeks, Romans, Celts, Normans, Vikings, the *Iliad*, *Odyssey*, Norse legends, the *Táin Bó Cuailgne*, *Beowulf*, *Macbeth*, *The Merchant of Venice*, poems and stories galore. We even had to write our own novel.

Everyone loved Carew's classes but Austin was in heaven. He gobbled up the work and begged for more. He was a real history freak. He wouldn't just tell you the life story of the guy who shot the arrow into King Harold's eye: he'd tell you the life stories of the birds whose feathers were used on the arrow.

The only subject he was bad at was P.E. but that didn't stop him knowing everything about sport. He'd know the wackiest facts, like who lost the mixed-doubles finals in Wimbledon in 1987.

After Darren, I suppose I was most friendly with him but we never saw him outside school hours. He lived miles away, two buses from the school. In Inchicore. And he was always in a tearing hurry to go home and get stuck into his homework.

That was first year. Second year was a different story. Mr Carew was on a career break. Instead of him we had three dumdaws. Mr Gormless Gormley for English; Mr O' Hanlon, our new form teacher, permanently emitting the signal 'don't bother me, I just want to drink coffee'. But then – disaster – Sad Case for history.

Sad Case was the school loo-la. His real name was Mr Cassidy but he'd always been called Sad Case, though it could just as well have been Bad Case or Mad Case.

He was old and grey, had mean little eyes, always wore the same grotty tweed jacket and hadn't a clue how to teach, which was sad when you realised he'd been a teacher for about thirty years. You could tell that he hated teaching, hated kids, hated everything about school. He'd have preferred to be a nightwatchman in a wax museum than a teacher who was meant to talk to kids. When you went into his room, he'd be slouched at his desk pretending to read. He never looked at us coming in. There was always litter on his floor, everything was shabby, loads of graffiti, masses of chewing-gum stuck on the edges of the tables not underneath like in all the other rooms. The tables were crammed together and Sad Case never bothered to straighten them out. He was always losing his temper and threatening terrible things about sending people to the principal. He never did, though, and I'd say the principal wouldn't have listened to him anyway. The atmosphere in his class was brutal, like eating burned porridge on a picnic or watching TV when the reception is wonky. You knew that nobody had enjoyed one of Sad Case's classes in years and he hadn't enjoyed one either. The only buzz you got in his room was when a wasp flew in by mistake.

He was rude too. 'Shut up, ya shower of tramps,' he'd say. 'You, over there, ya good-for-nothing lout without a brain in yer head, sit down and shut up.' He never knew our names. He just didn't bother to learn them.

Our very first Sad Case class was awful. He snarled and growled for the first five minutes then handed out grubby, graffiti-covered pages with the smudgy heading, 'First Year Revision Test'.

'I want to see if ye're as stupid as I've been told. Start working and not a sound out of ye.'

A minute later Austin put up his hand. 'Sir,' he said. 'Question two says "Norsemen". Shouldn't it be "Normans"?'

Sad Case glared at him. 'Put down your hand!' he snarled.

Austin was so surprised that he kept his hand up. 'Sir . . .' he started again.

'Put down your hand, I said!'

'Sir, the question is wrong.'

Sad Case's face was red and his glasses all steamed up.

'Are you starting, boy? Are you criticising my work?'

'No, sir.'

'Have you been listening to some of the older louts in this school, boy?'

The whole class was rigid, bricking. He was even madder than we'd expected.

'Answer me!'

'Yes, sir! I mean no, sir.' His voice was all squawky and wobbly.

Sad Case was leaning over Austin now, really bullying him.

'Keep your smart alec head down in my class.'

Austin bent his head and picked up his pen. Sad Case poked his shoulder.

'I'll be watching out for you, sonny. You'll learn a hard lesson from me yet.'

He stalked back to his desk.

'Back to work the rest of ye!' he roared. 'Do that test properly or there'll be trouble!'

We needn't have worried. We never saw the test again.

Afterwards, people were telling Austin to complain to Mr O'Hanlon but he just shrugged it off. 'There's no point,' he said. 'At all.'

Darren was hopping. 'The scumbag shouldn't get away with it!'

'What'll happen if I complain?' Austin bounced back. 'Nothing. Except Sad Case will have an even bigger grudge.'

'But . . .'

'Look, loads of people must have complained before and he's still here. So forget it.'

'You're yellow!' Darren jeered.

'Maybe.'

After that Austin kept his head down and so did the rest of us. And as the weeks passed, our heads went down, down, down. The only work we ever did was 'underlining' and worksheets. Underlining meant that Sad Case read out of our textbook and told us to underline the main parts. 'Underline from "In 1906" down to the end of the page,' he'd say. That might be most of the page. We'd actually have to underline it, not just draw a line in the margin. All just a way of passing the time.

Worksheets were worse. They were grubby and smudgy, typed on a bockety typewriter, full of head-wrecking, moronic questions.

'Full sentences!' he'd snarl. 'No lazy shortcuts!'

By mid-October, he hadn't corrected a single sentence. He'd never smiled, never complimented anyone. Although no one respected him, there was no talking or messing in his class. Everyone sat hunched up, saying nothing, learning nothing, wondering what the hell we were doing there, sending waves of hate towards Sad Case. If ill will could kill, he'd have been a goner long ago. Poor Austin was really suffering. On the days we had history, he always looked miserable, like a dog waiting to be kicked. And he was kicked. Sad Case never missed a chance to hassle him.

'You! Smart Alec! Is Paris in County Wexford?'

'No, sir.'

'Are you sure?'

'Yes, sir.'

'Was Napoleon a Chinaman?'

'No, sir.'

'Are you sure?'

Austin began to be absent more often. Migraine, he said. I think he'd have cracked up altogether if things had continued as they were. But they didn't.

Just before Hallowe'en Sad Case had set us a half-term test. The following day he was like an Antichrist, flapping our test papers, bawling about disgraceful work.

'Darren McMahon, zero out of twenty. Where are you, McMahon?'

Darren raised his hand.

'Stand up, you amadaun.'

Darren lumbered to his feet with a half-eejit grin on his face.

'What are you, McMahon?'

'Dunno, sir.'

'Dunno, thir,' he mimicked. 'An ignoramus, a gom, a galoot, a ludramaun? A Big Baluba, maybe?'

Poor Darren just stood there blushing, being spattered by Sad Case saliva.

'Well?'

'Sir, I dunno, sir.'

'Of course you don't know. Let's settle for Big Baluba. The alliteration is effective, isn't it, Big Baluba?' His bulgy eyes were about six inches from Darren's face. 'What is a Baluba?'

'Dunno, sir.'

'Of course you don't.' He pointed at Austin, sitting at the far side of the room. 'You! Smart Alec! Explain to McMahon here what a Baluba is.' Austin said nothing, just stared at his desk. Sad Case reddened. 'Stand up when I speak to you, you little scut!' he shouted.

No move from Austin.

'Stand up, I said! Or, by God, I'll make you stand!'

Almost lazily, Austin rose to his feet.

'Straighten up!'

Austin half straightened.

'Straighter!'

'Can't. I've a sore back.'

'I'll give you a sore back! Do you know what a Baluba is?'

'I do.'

'Tell McMahon, then.'

'Darren, the Balubas are an African tribe,' said Austin. He paused, then looked directly at Sad Case. 'And any teacher – especially an history teacher – who calls a pupil a Big Baluba can only be an ignorant, narrow-minded, bullying racist.'

Sad Case went ape. He roared, then lurched forward like a JCB on an awkward slope. He waded towards Austin through kids, schoolbags, tables, chairs but, before he reached him, Darren blocked his path.

'Get out of my way, you pup!' Sad Case snarled.

He caught Darren's arm and yanked him sideways. Austin dropped to his knees and, like a rabbit down a burrow, disappeared under the tables. Other kids were scrambling clear, overturning chairs, until we were all against the walls, a tangle of chairs between us and Sad Case. You'd think we were playing a crazy game of blindman's buff.

Sad Case was in a space of his own, heaving and swaying, like a mad buffalo about to charge. 'I'll . . . I'll . . . by God, I'll . . .' he was spluttering.

Then, like magic, Mr O'Hanlon was in the doorway, gawking at Sad Case, gawking at us.

After all the roaring, bawling and furniture moving, sudden, total silence. You could nearly hear hearts thumping. After ten forevers O'Hanlon cleared his throat. 'Em, may I have a word outside, Mr Cassidy?'

Sad Case no longer looked like a buffalo. He looked like a very bad version of himself. A wreck.

Still, he had one last hurrah. He waggled his finger at us all. 'A crowd of thugs, Mr O'Hanlon.' His voice was wobbly. 'A crowd of despicable, cowardly thugs. And him,' he pointed at Austin, 'the filthiest rat of them all.'

You could feel panic running through the class. Was he going to burst into tears? But he didn't. He spat. He hawked loudly, and a gobbet of snot arced through the air and plopped obscenely on the floor midway between him and us. Then he turned and shuffled out.

O'Hanlon looked like he'd been kicked where it hurt. He stared at the blob glistening vilely on the floor. 'I'll be back,' he croaked and hurried out.

No one said anything for a few seconds. Then sniggers, curses, deep breaths.

'That wasn't pretty,' someone said in a singsong voice and the sniggers became giggles.

Darren pushed his way close to Austin.

'Brainbox, you're some headcase! What you do that for?'

Austin was standing still, eyes half closed, his face a greenish colour.

'Fair dues, anyway, even if you are a headcase,' Darren said and slapped Austin on the back.

Austin staggered forwards and vomited a massive splurge of vomit all over Darren's schoolbag.

'Aw, Jaysis, Brainbox, that's me bag!'

Austin keeled over, whacking his head on a table.

None of us knew what to do except curse. But we were saved by O'Hanlon arriving again. The poor man was having a nightmare day. I bet he had a serious coffee binge that night. He told a couple of kids to bring Austin to the main office and he sent the rest of us to the canteen until it was time for our next class.

The day fizzled along uneasily after that. No sign of Austin or O'Hanlon. We were all waiting for lectures, interrogations, mass executions, but nothing happened. I reckon all our teachers knew about it but none of them said anything or hassled us at all. Forgotten textbooks, lousy homework didn't matter for once. Four o'clock came and we legged it fast, glad to be out of the place for a week. All during half-term I dreaded history but on the first day back O'Hanlon said that Mr Cassidy was unwell and wouldn't be in school in the short term. He didn't explain 'short term' and he didn't say anything about the hullabaloo. It was as if the school had decided that the best way to deal with it was to pretend it hadn't happened.

The only snag was that Austin wasn't back either. He was absent for the entire week and we were all wondering if he'd been expelled, or moved school or something.

Darren had a theory. 'Brain damage. Jaze, you'd be worried about Brainbox whacking his head the way he done. With a big brain like his, he could do a lot of damage. Looka this!' He headbutted the table viciously, then looked up at us, grinning. 'See? Felt nothin'. No brain, no damage.'

But the next Monday, there he was. At least, some of him was. Imagine opening an ice-cold can of Coke on a hot day and taking a great long swig from it. Imagine you were called away and when you came back, hours later, there was the Coke, all lukewarm and flat. That was the difference in Austin. Dull, flat, no chat, no jokes, as if he'd had part of his brain removed.

Like an eejit, I waded straight in as soon as I saw him.

'Hey, Austin! Thought you'd been snapped up by Man. U.'

'Hmm?'

'Were you sick?'

'Sort of.'

'Headaches?'

'Sort of.'

'What your folks say about Sad Case?'

'Not much. Better go to my locker.'

That was the end of that. It was like wading through seaweed.

Leave him alone, I thought, he'll cheer up in a few days. But he didn't, not that day or that week or even all that term. He was 'like an oul' pair of drawers with the elastic gone' as Mr Carew used to say about our class when we had no energy. He didn't smile or tell jokes, in class he didn't ask questions. He started going to the library at lunchtime instead of hanging round with the usual gang. Maybe Darren was right about the brain damage.

We had free history classes for a few days, then this new teacher, Mr Murray, marched in unannounced and said, 'RIGHT! There's a lot of history to learn! The entire history of the human race to begin with! Off with the coats, out with the pens! Let's waste no time!' We went straight into the Russian Revolution and how the sad old Tsar got chucked out. Very appropriate really.

You'd think that Austin would've brightened up now that we'd a good history teacher again, but he didn't. He still got top marks in tests but he never asked questions or showed much interest in what we were doing. He looked as though he had a permanent headache, pale and peaky and squinty.

After six weeks of Mr Murray, Sad Case was starting to seem like a bad dream.

Darren and I were talking about him one morning on our way to school.

'I heard he's in a loony bin,' Darren said.

'Who said?'

'Just heard.'

'Could be.'

'Put him out with the rubbish, they should.'

We heard a shout behind us. 'Lads! Leds! Stall it!' It was Austin, bursting himself to catch us.

'What's up?' Darren asked.

'Guess what?' Austin was all bright eyed and excited.

'What?'

'He's coming back.'

'Who?'

'I met Mr Carew . . .'

'Carew? Where?'

'In town. I'd a big chat with him. He knew all about it. He's a friend of Cassidy's.'

'What?'

'Mr Cassidy. Sad Case. Carew said he's much better. He'll be back after Christmas.'

Darren caught hold of Austin's jacket. 'Brainbox, who's comin' back? Sad Case or Carew?'

'Sad Case, of course. Mr Carew is doing an M.Ed. in Trinity. He . . .'

Darren gave him a shake. 'Brainbox, you're talkin' to

Darren here, remember? What's so bleedin' brilliant about Sad Case comin' back?'

'I'm just glad he is, OK?'

'Why?'

'Look, you were there that day . . .'

'Bleedin' sure I was an' I'm not bleedin' glad he's comin' back.'

Austin was getting himself into a right twist. 'It's hard to explain. Look, I didn't like to think . . . I know he was messed up but I didn't want to be the one . . . Anyway, I'll see yis later!'

He broke away from us and dashed towards the school with his skinny-legged scuttle of a run. Darren and I stood looking after him.

'He'll never play for Man. United,' I said.

Darren shook his head. 'He's some freak, that Brainbox, isn't he? Jaze, I'm glad I'm thick.'

True Believers

Joseph O'Connor

When I was seven years old – in the winter before my mother went away to England and the life of my family was changed forever – we knew an old woman called Agnes Bernadette Graham. She went to the same church as us, Holy Family Glasthule. That was how we met her, and that was where we continued to meet her for a time, which I suppose was about a year, every Sunday, after that first time.

Glasthule, in Irish, means 'the green apple', so that at an early age the name of this place got mixed up in my head with the story of Adam and Eve, the forbidden fruit, the lush garden of innocence, and how it was a woman who had brought sin into the previously perfect world. When my parents were fighting each other in the kitchen, I used to sit with my little sisters Miriam and Ruth in our big back garden, in the hut that my father had built for us, talking about these things. Because we were children, and because we had nothing better to do, we would imagine together what Eden must have been like.

Ruth said it was probably like Disneyland, full of swimming pools and chocolate streams and castles made of ice. Miriam said it was a place where you got three wishes to start every day. You could use these three wishes to wish for more wishes. And you could use those wishes to wish for even more. You could keep going like this for all eternity, until you had a mountain of wishes, more wishes than you would ever be able to count, never mind use. In Eden, you could have even done this, if that's what you wanted to do.

At that time I used to go to church with my father and Ruth and Miriam, and my little brother, Max. Back then, Max was still just a toddler. He used to sing in his cot at night, a song that went 'Here comes the fire brigade, dar, dar, dar', over and over again, with no other words apart from these.

I was the eldest child of my parents' marriage, so I was the only one of us who could remember back to a time when they did not fight each other. I could also remember praying to Jesus to send Max to us, because I was so sick of having sisters. I wanted a little brother to talk to, and to teach him how to spell, something I enjoyed doing, and something that was easy enough for me. In later years when Max got into trouble, which he did very often, I used to remind him about this. I used to tell him that if it wasn't for me, he wouldn't have ever got here. Long after I stopped believing in God, I never quite stopped believing that my brother Max was something out of the ordinary, because I had wanted him so very much, in the way that children sometimes do.

The first day we met Agnes was a Sunday, a very cold Sunday in the winter of what must have been 1971. That was the kind of day where your breath turns to steam when you breathe. Or smoke, if you are a child. That is what you think, anyway. You are at the age when you can see the magic in the most ordinary things.

I remember it was so icy that morning that my father and I could not go to play on the little putting green next to the church, something that we almost always did after Mass, while my sisters went to get the papers. My father would show me how to hold the club, how to go down on my hunkers and judge the curve of the ground, how to draw an invisible line from the end of the putter to the exact centre of the hole. But the ground was too hard that morning, so the putting green was closed, the little clubhouse was locked, and the rusty, blue metal flags had been taken out of the holes and put away. When you stamped on the grass, it felt crisp. Underneath that, the earth felt like stone.

So we were just standing in front of the church on that freezing morning, the five of us, my father and Ruth and Miriam and I, and Max in my father's arms, each of us blowing on our thumbs and wondering what we could do. Because although we were too young to be able to admit something like this, we did not want to go home. We did not want that at all. This was because the worst fights in our house were always on a Sunday. And they always ended with my father putting on his jacket and leaving our house, and not coming back until it was late, and we were in bed, and school was just a few short hours away.

My father looked at me that morning, and I could see by the look on his face that he knew what I was thinking. His lips were cracked and pale, and he kept chewing at the skin there, while he stared around himself, at the trees in the churchyard, and up at the sky, as though he was waiting for some strange thing to happen to him.

'Daddy,' said Ruth, 'I'm cold.'

'I know you are, sweetie,' my father said, 'but think of the people in Africa, in the desert. Think how they'd like to be here now.'

'I don't care about the people in Africa,' said Ruth, 'I wish I was there now, instead of here.' My father laughed, softly.

'So do I,' he said, 'if you want to know the truth.'

We stood in front of the church until all the people had gone home, and the newspaper man had packed up his stall, and the young priest had gone through the front gates of the church, clapping his hands together, and into the little house that he had across the road. And I can remember wishing then that I too was a priest, and had a warm house to go to, where there would be no parents, no brother and sisters, no spouse, no one to love and cause you the trouble that this involves.

'Hell with it,' my father said suddenly, 'I feel like an adventure today. Let's just jump in the car and take off somewhere.'

'Do you mean it?' we said.

''Course I mean it,' he beamed, 'let's go cause a bit of mischief somewhere.'

'Brillo,' yelled Miriam.

'Gear,' said Ruth.

'Rapid,' I said.

We thought this was fine. Now we would not have to go home until four or five o'clock. Now there would not be as much time for them to fight each other. My father lifted Max high in the air and he laughed.

'Come on, boy,' he said, 'what do you say?'

'Here comes the fire brigade,' said Max, 'dar, dar, dar.'

And I remember feeling the most intense happiness right then. I remember thinking that this would be a good day now, a day when everything might well work out to be all right.

And just as we were walking around the church to get to the car park at the back, I remember being so happy that I began to run. I skidded on the ice, sprinted ahead, right around the corner as hard as I could, with Ruth and Miriam chasing after me, throwing stones, screeching.

'Come back here,' my father shouted, 'please, for God's sake, can't you behave just once.'

And that was when I saw something weird.

At first I thought she was dead. Down beside the gable wall of the church, beside the big black plastic bin where they kept the holy water, I saw this little clump of black clothing which contained an old woman.

She lay flat on her back, with her arms extended on each side of her tiny body. Her eyes were closed. Her legs were thin and crooked. Her skin was white. She lay so still that I can clearly remember thinking to myself, 'This woman is dead, and what should we do now?'

Beside her, on the ground, was an empty 7-Up bottle. It rolled backwards and forwards, and it spun on the smooth ice. My father struggled around the corner with Max in his arms, cursing. For a moment he just looked at the old woman too. Then he spoke.

'Oh my God,' he said, 'that poor woman is after slipping on the ice.'

My father put Max into my arms, and I could barely hold him because he was so fat, and because he began to scream and kick his podgy legs. 'Shut up, Max,' I said, 'shut up, you big eejit.'

My father walked over very carefully to where the old woman was. He put his hands in his pockets. He looked over his shoulder, but nobody was coming to help him. He stared down at her, then he said 'Hello, hello?' in a cautious voice, as though this old woman was a wild animal who might wake up and turn on him at any minute. We crept up behind my father, laughing a little, enjoying the terror of what might be about to happen. For a moment we stood there, giggling, and I could feel my heart beginning to pound. Then I stepped in front of my father and I saw the old woman's bleeding head. It turned, on the ground. It opened its eyes. It looked at us.

Nobody seemed to be able to think of anything to say. So I took another step forward and I said, 'So, what's your name?'

She looked up at me then. She smiled. She said, 'Love, my name is Agnes, and I am the lamb of God.' Then she started to cry. I think she had just taken a fright, all of a sudden. She seemed to be confused and shaken up, and not to know where she was any more. She opened her mouth to cry and her false teeth nearly fell out. She clamped her hand to her lips, and sobbed like a baby. My father held her in his arms. He stroked the back of her head. 'Where am I?' she said. 'What's happening to me now?'

'You're safe now, missus,' my father said, 'you're in the Holy Family church. You're OK. Nothing can happen to you here.' Slowly we helped Agnes to her feet. Her old black coat smelt dirty. She looked around, squinting her eyes, sniffing. She told my father that she had been stretching up to get some holy water from the bin, when she had turned her ankle on the ice. 'You poor thing,' he said, 'you have to be on the look-out for that in this weather.'

My father started to fuss then. He put his hand on Agnes's forehead and he made her count his fingers. He said he wanted to get a doctor, or take Agnes to a hospital. But she shook her head and said she was fine now. She kept looking at my father, holding her hand over her forehead to stop the glare that was coming off the ice, wrinkling her nose as she stared at him. She gazed at his face, as though my father was somebody she recognised, but whose name she could not remember.

'There is one thing you could do for me,' she said then, and she picked up the empty 7-Up bottle. She waved the bottle in front of herself, and she nodded in the direction of the holy water bin.

'Oh,' said my father, 'of course.' He took the bottle, reached into the bin, broke the ice with his fist and filled it up. She smiled when he gave the bottle back to her. And I noticed that for some reason my father was blushing. 'Now,' he said, 'you're set up.' He handed her the bottle and rubbed his hands on his coat.

'Yes, I am,' she said, 'I'm laughing now.'

We gave Agnes a lift home that day, to the little street full of corporation houses where she lived. The street was dirty and there was a burnt-out car down against the wall of the flats, beside a big spraypaint sign that said 'UP THE PROVOS' and another one that said 'PHILIP LYNOTT RULES OK'. Agnes said she'd have liked to invite us in for a cup of something, but the house was all upside down, so, if we didn't mind. No, my father told her, of course we didn't mind in the least. I was disappointed. I would have loved to see inside the house of this strange, smelly old woman.

From then on I used to look forward to seeing Agnes at Mass every Sunday. In the garden Miriam said she was a witch, but I paid no attention to that. I liked Agnes. She was full of strange stories, and just the way she put things was pretty weird. But Miriam didn't like her at all. She said Agnes was a cannibal. She said the reason Agnes wouldn't allow us into her house was that she killed babies in there, and ate them, and made tomato ketchup out of their blood and bones. I knew that this was not true, but I made up my mind to keep an eye on the way she looked at Max in future.

Little by little we got to know Agnes well. She was always curious about our lives, what we were doing in school, what we wanted to be when we grew up. And sometimes she was curious about our mother too. She asked about her a lot, in those early days, when we met her first.

'She must be very proud of such a lovely family,' she'd say, 'she must thank God.'

My father would go quiet then, and say,

'Well of course, we're both very proud, Rita and me too. They're brats, of course, but they're good kids really.'

He told Agnes that my mother preferred to get Mass in Sallynoggin or Killiney, and we never contradicted him. The truth was that my mother had already stopped going to Mass by then. The way things turned out, she never did meet Agnes. That's a pity. They would have got on well together. I once told my mother about Agnes. I said that my father was very kind to her.

'Oh, is he?' she said. 'Well, he should realise that charity begins at home.'

But later that night my mother came into my room. She sat on my bed for a while, smoking a cigarette, and she said that she hadn't meant what she'd said about my father, and that my father was a good man, and that she did not want for me to turn against him, in case I would grow up unhappy, and never want to get married myself.

My mother was not religious at all. She said religion was all lies and hypocrisy and it brought out the worst of the great bitterness that was in her. She said she wasn't biased, she hated all religions equally. Agnes was different, of course, but one odd thing, she hated priests. She said they were parasites and fools who were polluting the word of God and living it up like dukes. She had that quality of intolerance wrapped up in resignation that you only ever find in very religious people. I used to hear her during the sermon, clicking her tongue, scoffing in the seats behind us where she always sat now. She said things like 'That's a good one coming from him', and 'A lot he'd know about the will of God'.

Agnes had never got married. When we asked her why, she used to tell us that she was still waiting for the right fellow. Then she'd quake with laughter, wiping her eyes, and she'd say, 'Oh God forgive me!' She'd say that a lot.

One day she showed me a picture of the Sacred Heart, with his eyes flaring with passion, and his chest all bleeding.

'See him?' she said to me. 'That's the only boyfriend I'll ever have.' Other times she used to say that all men were the same and she wasn't one bit sorry to be on her own. I think she had quite a thing for my father though. 'If only,' she used to smirk, 'if only you were fifty years older.'

'Oh, now Agnes,' he'd say, 'you're an awful woman, putting temptation in my way. You're a Jezebel, Agnes Graham, and me a happily married man.'

She would laugh then, and so would he. And we would laugh too, in the back seat of the car, even though we didn't actually know what a Jezebel was.

Then one night when we were sitting on the landing, listening to them fight each other downstairs, I heard my father call my mother that.

'You're a hypocrite, and you're weak,' she told him.

'And you're a backstabbing, Jezebel witch,' he shouted. She cried then. So did he. We could hear them, crying downstairs, in separate rooms now. I knew what it meant then all right.

I promised myself that when I grew up, I would never use that word to anybody. I did not realise that when people are in love with each other, they are capable of anything. This was because I was a child. I was too young to see that.

We never found out what Agnes's age was.

'Thirty-nine,' she'd say, whenever we asked her. She thought this was just hilarious. She'd just fall around the place at that one. But my father told me once that she'd said she could remember the death of Queen Victoria, in 1901. So allowing that she might have been nine or ten then, this would have made her maybe eighty years old in 1971, the eventful year when we met her.

Agnes had this big thing about the devil. She talked about him all the time. She told us one day what she used to do with all the holy water that she brought home from the church. She used it to ward off the devil. She poured it all over everything in her house, to keep the devil away from her. She held up her Coca-Cola bottle, full of holy water, and she shook it hard.

'Oh, this is the real thing all right,' she cackled, 'I always keep a bottle of this in the house, for when his nibs comes calling on me.'

She drenched her clothes and her bedsheets with this magical water. She drank it, cooked her food in it. Whenever she bathed – which Ruth said mustn't have been too often – she filled her bath with it. She doused it all over the furniture and up and down the stairs. She said she could see the devil's eyes at night, coming in through the curtains. Big bright eyes, like Tyrone Power, and a voice, she said, like fingernails on a slate. He was coming to drag her off to hell because she was such a wicked woman. He kept coming to tempt her, offering her all manner of wickedness, if she would only give him her soul. My father had no tolerance for this.

'Now don't be silly, Agnes,' he'd say, 'don't be frightening the children.' But Agnes would insist.

'It's true,' she'd say, 'child, woman or man, it makes no difference to the prince of darkness.'

'There's no such thing as hell,' my father snapped one day, with anger in his eyes.

'Well, that's where you're wrong,' Agnes said, 'there is so a hell, and I have seen it.'

'When,' I said, 'when did you see hell?'

'Jesus showed it to me,' she said, 'a great big lake of fire and ice, and the awful screams of the damned echoing around the sky.'

'I don't believe you,' said my father, 'that's just rubbish.'

'Oh is it?' shouted Agnes. 'Is it now? Well, I'm a true believer, my lad, and on the day of judgement we'll see who's so smart.'

My father told us not to pay any attention to her. He said Agnes was a madwoman who should be locked up somewhere. And the next week at Mass he did not speak to her. I felt sorry for Agnes, standing beside the holy water bin, all alone, peering at us when she thought my father was not looking.

The Sunday after that she came up to us in the car park with four stale cakes, wrapped in a piece of newspaper. She said she had missed us very much and had been praying for us all. My father looked cross. But when he saw the cakes, wrapped up in the newspaper, his face softened and he smiled. He said that we had missed her too.

'You can give me a lift home so,' she said, 'I've grown accustomed to the style.'

Things continued in this manner throughout that year, with nothing of great importance happening between Agnes and us. We would meet her outside the church, talk for a while, sometimes go for an ice-cream in the Blue Moon Café, then bring her home to her house. Agnes became a part of our lives. I think we just got used to Agnes, and she got used to us. She gave us religious pictures on our birthdays, and she always remembered to send her regards to our mother. In the back garden, we wondered how much Agnes knew about us, whether the devil really did come to haunt her every night, and if she was some kind of weird magician who could see into the secret part of our lives.

I remember the day of my eighth birthday fell on a Sunday that year. After Mass, Agnes took me to one side and gave me a little parcel, wrapped in blue and silver paper. It was a set of black rosary beads, with 'Welcome to Knock' written on the medal.

'Thank you very much, Agnes,' I said. She smiled at me. Then she touched my face with her fingers.

'You're the eldest,' she said, 'that's a cross, love, I know that, and Jesus knows it too.' The way she looked at me made it impossible to look away. 'Pray to the Holy Family,' she whispered, 'they will see you right.'

'I will, Agnes,' I said, and I wanted to cry.

'You just be a true believer, pet,' she said, 'and everything will turn up smelling of roses, you'll see.'

Agnes kissed me then. She had a moustache. Her hands were like claws. She said I was handsome, like my father, and that when I grew up I would break somebody's heart.

Then I remember another special day, in the summer of 1972, the twenty-seventh of August. We all went out to Bray after Mass, again, my father and me, my sisters and Agnes and Max. We left my mother at home, the way we always did. Agnes was so excited that her face went all red, and we laughed at her until my father said he'd stop the car and slap our legs if we didn't stop.

It was a wonderful day. The sky was clear and the sea was all a weird shade of blue, like the colour of the stuff you put on your knees when you scrape them. Down by the pier the bumper cars and slot machines were rattling, and the sea horses raced in across the waves to the beach. Agnes said the waves were the souls of the angels that God really loved. She said God let them dance about on the sea for all eternity as a reward for their goodness. Some reward, Miriam said.

We walked up Bray Head. And no matter how much my father fretted, Agnes insisted on going all the way to the top. She wanted to see the big black cross at the summit. We had to stop every twenty yards for Agnes to catch her breath. On the way up the winding path people glared at my father, and they whispered and pointed. I think they thought that he was forcing this poor old woman to climb all the way up this terrible hill. They didn't realise it was her idea. I felt ashamed. I walked in front so that nobody would know Agnes had anything to do with me.

'This was the best day ever,' Agnes sighed, getting out of the car. 'I haven't had a day like this since 1957.'

'Our pleasure, Agnes,' my father smiled, 'we'll do it again some time soon.'

But as we drove up the hill and home that day, my father could not have known that days like this would not happen again, and that everything in his life was about to be changed.

When we got home our house was empty and the phone was off the hook. When I walked into the hall I could hear the tone, growling. I picked up the receiver and held it to my ear. The noise made me think of some animal, but I did not know which one. Ruth came from the kitchen with the note in her hands.

She said, 'Daddy, I think Mammy's gone.'

'Don't be silly,' my father laughed, 'she's gone out for a message.' He took off his coat and hung it across the back of a chair.

'No,' said Ruth, 'you're wrong.' She gave him the note that she had found by the fridge. She was crying now.

The note said that my mother had taken enough, and

that she had to get away for some peace. 'I will always love you all,' it said, 'but I cannot go on with a life like this.'

My father stared at this note for some time, holding it very lightly in his hands, as though it was on fire. He sat down on the stairs, and he read it again. Then he looked at us, and he spoke.

'It's just a joke,' my father whispered. He crumpled up the note and he laughed, and then he threw the paper on the floor, and then he went to the bathroom.

I was not very upset. I knew my father was, but I could not see why. All I could see was that now there would be no more fights. When you are the age that I was then, you do not realise the pain of being left, or the pain of leaving either. You are just too young to know about these things.

When Ruth and Miriam had stopped crying that night, my father went out to get chips and hamburgers. He was gone for a long time. When he came back he had a smell of beer on his breath and the chips were almost cold. He told us that a funny thing had happened. He had run into one of my mother's friends at the chip shop, and she had told him my mother was just gone away for a little holiday.

'So you see?' he smiled. 'I told you there was nothing to worry about.' He put the chips out on to plates and he looked me in the eye. 'You believe that,' he said, 'don't you, son?'

'Yes,' I said, 'I believe it.'

'That's good,' he said, 'that's very good, son. I mean, you know your dad wouldn't lie to you, don't you?'

'Yes,' I said, 'I know you wouldn't do that.' And I was happy then, because I knew I had said what my father wanted me to say.

We soldiered on regardless, as my father put it. At night he would sit by the telephone, waiting, just waiting, for it to ring. When I asked him who he was waiting for, he would look up from his newspaper and smile and say, 'Oh, just Uncle Joe', or 'Grandad' or 'Someone from the office'.

And then my father started coming home early from work so that he would be there when we got off school. He said he didn't want to send us out in the mornings with a key-chain round our necks. For the first few weeks we ate Kentucky Fried Chicken and takeaway pizza. Then my father began to learn to cook, out of a book he bought one Saturday. He burned all our pots and put flour in the meringues. Ruth said that our mother was never coming back now.

'You shouldn't come home so much,' I told him, 'we can look after ourselves.'

'Don't you worry about that,' he smiled, 'I like coming home early. It gives me a chance to catch up on the garden.' Every day we found him there at four o'clock, raking, cutting the grass, trimming the edges of the flowerbeds, until our garden was almost too beautiful to play in any more. He took us to the garden centre and we bought an apple tree. The day he planted it, he came into the kitchen, drenched in sweat, and he drank a pint of milk in three gulps. Looking at him, I could suddenly see that he didn't look like our father any more. He wiped his face with his vest. He leaned his hand on the kitchen table, and he looked around the room, as though he had never been there before in his life. He looked like a tired man, who needed to sleep for a week. 'God, I love doing that garden,' he said, 'we've really let it go over the last few years.'

One day not long after that, I found a letter in my father's bedroom, from his boss. It said that the company understood there were domestic difficulties, but his sales rate was well down, and if my father's performance did not improve, they would have to let him go. We sold the car soon after that, and from then on we walked down to Mass every Sunday, and I pushed Max in his pram.

'Never fear,' my father said, 'the walking is good for us anyway.'

One Sunday morning Agnes did not come to Mass. We looked all over the church for her, but she wasn't there. So after church we didn't bother getting the newspaper. And we didn't bother to play putting, because my father had told me in secret that we couldn't really afford it any more, not for the moment, not until our fortunes began to change again. Instead we decided to go call on Agnes, just to make sure that she was all right. We walked all together down the back streets to the little cul-de-sac where she lived. It didn't take very much time, because I knew a short cut. My father held the girls' hands and he laughed.

'Your brother has a sense of direction,' he said, 'that's a useful thing to have in life.'

Outside Agnes's house there were four bottles of milk on the step. One of them was cracked. The birds had pecked the foil off the tops. My father rang the doorbell, but nobody came. That didn't matter. Agnes was a little deaf, he said. He pressed the doorbell again, hard, and he rapped on the door with his fingers. Still nobody came.

I stood on tiptoe and stared through Agnes's letterbox. But she had one of those metal boxes on the inside of her door to stop the skinheads throwing rubbish through the letterbox, so I couldn't see a thing.

My father banged on the window with his wedding ring. The curtains were closed. He turned and smiled at us. Then he banged the glass again, so hard that I thought he would break it, and get into some kind of trouble.

All the boys stood leaning with their backs against the wall, just watching us. They had a radio. It went 'Saturday, Saturday, Saturday night's all right for fighting'. One of them was pretending to play the electric guitar. His eyes were closed and he shook his long hair. The others, his friends, just kept staring. Ruth said she wanted to go home. She said she didn't like being here, didn't like it one bit. I told her to shut up. My father bit his upper lip between his teeth. He started to walk up and down outside Agnes's house, running his fingers through his hair. And all of a sudden my father looked like a child. Or a man who was lost. Or a man in a fairy-tale who had found himself in a strange situation, one that he couldn't understand at all.

'Something's wrong,' he kept saying, 'something is not right here.' He punched the wall, gently, with his fist. He ran his finger around the inside of his collar. He stared down at the milk bottles, lined up outside Agnes's door. He glanced at his watch, then at me, then at his watch again.

My father looked me in the eye. He smiled. Then very suddenly the expression on his face darkened. He grabbed me by the shoulders. He said that I had to go knock on all the doors in the street, find someone who had a telephone, call an ambulance. I had to be responsible now. I had to act like a man. I told him I didn't want to. I didn't want to knock on the doors of these dirty little houses where people were going to laugh at me.

My father took his hands from my shoulders.

'Shame on you,' he said in a hoarse voice, and then he turned to Ruth and Miriam. 'Girls,' he said, 'your dad needs you to help him.'

'All right,' I said, 'I'll do it.'

'No, no,' he said, 'if your dad can't rely on you, that's just fine, I'll remember that.'

'Please,' I said, 'let me do it. I want to do it.'

'Go on, then,' he said, 'just get out of my sight.'

I did it. I walked all the way down one side of the street and all the way back up the other, and I knocked on every door.

At last I found a woman who didn't have a phone exactly, but she called her husband out from where he was eating his breakfast and told him to run to the pub and get help. I ran down the street after him, trying to keep up. And now there was a crowd of people outside Agnes's house.

The radio was still going. 'Saturday night's all right,' it said, 'Saturday night's all right for fighting.' Ruth was sitting on the kerb, with her coat up over her head. Miriam was trying to look through the front window. Max was crawling in the gutter. As I walked over I saw one man in the crowd take off his hat. I heard a dry mumbling sound, coming from Agnes's hall. It was a sound that I recognised. It was a sound that I had heard many times in my life, and one that I would never hear again. It was the sound of a group of people praying.

I pushed my way in past the smashed planks of the front door. The smell made me want to be sick. From the top of the stairs I saw a big black cat staring down at me. It had bright yellow eyes. It licked its lips and yawned, and it rubbed its back against the banister.

My father was standing in the front room with his back to me. With his right hand he was clutching his left shoulder. With his left hand he was holding a handkerchief over his mouth and nose. A small, frightened-looking man who I did not recognise was standing beside my father, with an axe in his hands. His face was white. His lips were moving, but no sound was coming from his mouth.

The floor was thick with dirty yellow newspapers. The room stank of rot and mould and piss. On the wall, a painting of the Virgin Mary in a blue cloak smiled down, with her hands extended, and beams of light coming from every finger.

In front of my father and the man with the axe, I could see that there was a mattress, stretched out in a corner of the room. As I walked around my father, he put his hand on my shoulder. His hands were shaking. He did not look at me.

Agnes was lying on this mattress, in her old black coat, with some kind of torn-up nightdress underneath. Her eyes were open. Her lips were blue. Her tongue was sticking out of her mouth. It was black. Flies were crawling across her face. Her hands were folded across her breasts, and she was holding an empty bottle. Above the mattress were some words, scribbled onto the flower patterned wallpaper with a crayon. 'Oh, most Sacred Heart of Jesus,' they said, 'I place all my trust in thee.'

My father pulled me to him for a moment. He held me very tight and then he made me turn away.

'Go take care of your sisters and Max,' he whispered, 'this isn't something you want to see.' And when I turned away from him, that was when I saw them. The bottles.

On the floor. On the table. Lined up on the bookshelf and the windowsill. Under the bed. In the sink and the cooker in every cupboard in the kitchen. All the way up the stairs. My feet kicked against them, sent them tumbling down the steps and into the street. In the bath, and around the toilet. In every filth-encrusted room, hundreds and hundreds and thousands of bottles, some full, some empty, some wriggling with fat maggots and beetles. Coke bottles, sherry bottles, marmalade jars, milk bottles, plastic bottles from Lourdes shaped like the Virgin Mary. An army of bottles, in every corner of Agnes Bernadette Graham's tiny house.

The doctor said it was the damp. Everything in the house was soaked through. It was staggering, he said. It was just no way for anyone to have to live. He pulled the dirty sheet up over Agnes's head, and he sat on the mattress beside her holding her hand as though she was still alive, waiting for the ambulance to come.

Agnes Graham died of pneumonia, convinced that she

was a sinner for whom the gates of hell were yawning. Sometimes when we spoke about her in our garden, I could see the look that would come over her innocent and strange face when she raved about the devil, and the furnaces of hell and the screams of the damned, and the indelible blackness of her soul. It was a look that I recognised again when I saw her lying cold and dead on that Sunday morning, her body twisted and stiff, with only her legion of bottles to mourn her. It was a look of the most ineffable fear.

Not many people came to her funeral. Just me and my father, and Miriam and Ruth, and a young, pretty woman we did not know, who said that Agnes had once done her a great kindness, but that she did not want to talk about it. It was a beautiful sunny day, but very windy, so that the priest's white vestments kept blowing into his face. My father gave a five-pound note to the gravediggers, because he said that digging graves was hard work, and a task that was not easy for anyone to do. They said they were sorry for his trouble, and he nodded, and shook their hands.

The night of Agnes's funeral I could not sleep. That was, if my memory is reliable, maybe five months after my mother had finally gone away from us.

When I came down the stairs it was late. My father was sitting in the front room, in an armchair, still wearing his black suit. His shoes were off, and his toes were sticking through his socks. My father was crying. His hands were touching his face, and he was softly saying some words to himself, over and over again. And the words he was saying through his tears – 'Rita, oh Rita, oh Rita' – were the words of my mother's name.

This was not the first time I had seen my father cry. But it was the worst time. He sat with his head in his hands, almost as though he was going to suddenly open his fingers and go 'Boo!!' He sat very still, sobbing, breathing very hard, saying my mother's name over and over again, as though her name was a poem, or a prayer. And I knew that this time my father was not playing.

Then I wanted to cry too. Not just because I was upset, but because I wanted to cry with my father. I did not want him to have to cry on his own. I wanted to hold him, and for him to hold me, and I wanted to cry in his arms until all of our tears had cried themselves out and gone away. I could see in that moment that my father was entitled to cry. And I wanted to cry too, but I found that I could not.

That was the night my childhood ended. Because when you feel this feeling for your parents – that they, like you, are entitled to cry – you know that you yourself are not a child any more.

And this was also the night that God died in my life. I found myself in a new world, into which death had come, a world in which death was now a possibility, and a fact which seemed to change the way I saw everything, in an instant of time, the way the most major changes of your life can happen, in a manner that you would think would not be important at all.

Later that night my father and I went to the kitchen and we broke two hamburgers off the block in the freezer, fried them with bread, and sat in the front room watching *Starsky and Hutch* on the TV. He drank a can of beer and I drank milk. He kept wiping his eyes with his tie. Whenever he finished a cigarette, he lit another one on the end.

'I suppose you think your dad is an awful man now,' he said, 'I suppose you think he's nothing but a baby.'

'No,' I said, 'that's not what I think.'

'Yes, well don't you worry anyway,' he kept saying to me, 'you're too young to worry about the big things. We'll just keep the flag flying here, and things will work out for the best.'

'I won't worry,' I said, 'I promise.'

'That's good, son,' he said, and he sighed. 'One lesson you learn,' he said, 'things don't get any easier, no matter what people believe.' He crushed his beer can and put it on the floor, by his seat.

'I'll remember that,' I said, and he laughed out loud, and his face brightened, and he said he was happy to hear it.

We sat in silence for some minutes, listening to the rain that was beginning to fall now, softly against the windows of our house. Somewhere out on the street a burglar alarm was wailing, and all the dogs were barking at the thunder.

My father looked at me, and he tried to smile, although the tears were beginning once more to trickle down his face.

'Did I ever tell you,' my father said, suddenly, 'that sometimes you look just like your mother did, when she was young, and we fell in love together?'

'No,' I said, 'you never did.'

My father bent his forehead, and he pinched the bridge of his nose. He sat like that for a short time, and I watched him, until slowly he raised his head again, and he wiped his nose on the back of his sleeve, and he looked into my eyes in a way I had never seen before. He nodded once or twice.

'No,' he said quietly, 'well, you do.'

And we sat in each other's arms then, until the television ended, and the National Anthem played. We listened to the sound of the rain for a while, hissing into our garden. I suppose we must have wondered about all manner of things, but I do not remember that. All I remember is the sound of the rain, and that I held on to my father very hard, his smell, the strength of his shoulders, the solid and lonely beat of his true-believing heart.

Icepick Murphy and the Durango Kid

Herbie Brennan

There was a whole gang of us used to gruel round the estate when we were little, but most of them drifted away. Tommy

Connor's auld ones upped and took him to Australia. Your man Shay Farr – the one that dressed up as Superdog with a cape made out of a towel – went into the borstal and we never saw him again. I don't know where Willie O'Leary got to at all. He was older than the rest of us and he just disappeared. By the time I was ten, half the crowd was gone and by the time I was thirteen, there was only Icepick and me left.

Icepick was called Icepick because he said he'd beat the tar out of anybody who called him by his real name. His real name was Ignatius, after the saint. Ignatius Murphy. Can you credit any mother inflicting that on her son? When he was about seven or maybe eight, he sneaked into an 18s movie at the Carlton in O'Connell Street and the villain did in nuns with an icepick. Icepick's been Icepick ever since.

I never minded my name, but a quilt up from Kerry said I reminded him of the Durango Kid and it stuck. I didn't know who the Durango Kid was and neither did my ma, but when the grandda came out of hospital he said it was this character from the old cowboy pictures. Used to wear a hat and ride a white horse like the Loan Arranger. God knows how the quilt got me out of that, but he's rotting back in Kerry now, so I never had the chance to ask him.

The place we grew up was the Ballyfarther council estate. The 'bally' comes from *baile*, which means 'town' in Irish, so I suppose the whole place was a town on its own at one time. But it's a part of Dublin now. You can find it easy enough. Just stand anywhere in Ireland and keep walking in the most miserable direction. You'll end up in Ballyfarther.

'Ballyfarther?' my grandma used to say after the third or fourth stout. 'The farther the better if you ask me.' Then she'd cackle with her mouth open so her top set fell down on the bottom with this big bubbly click. It was desperate.

I expect 'farther' means something else in Irish, but the Brothers never got me beyond *baile* for all they tried to stuff the language into me. I'd no head for it at all. But I agreed with Grandma even though the click of her false teeth made me feel sick.

The trick was to get away from Ballyfarther. The farther the better. Tommy Connor's auld ones knew all about that – you can't get much farther than Australia. But my ma was afraid to walk as far as Grafton Street and my da was having a great time in the army at the Curragh Camp, so what did he care? If I wanted to leave, I'd have to do it myself. I suppose that's why I ever listened to Icepick.

'It's all money,' Icepick said.

'What is?' I asked him.

'Life,' says he, just like an auld one. We were both mitching school and walking down by the canal, not because we liked it, but because nobody ever thought of looking for us there. Besides, everybody threw their old Lotto tickets over the bridge and a couple of times we'd found one that hadn't been drawn yet. I suppose they got threw over by somebody the worse for drink. Not that we won anything, but it was a bit of excitement and we lived in hope. 'Life,' he says again. Then he looks at me directly. 'You and me could have a great time if we had money.'

No arguing with that, so I didn't. 'Where would you and me get money?' I asked him. I had twenty pence in the back pocket. Icepick had less. I knew that because he wanted some off me earlier. He had this idea we'd have an ice-cream at Cafolla's. Like we could even afford to phone Cafolla's.

'I've been thinking about that,' he said.

Turned out what he was thinking about was robbing.

'That's what got Shay Farr into the borstal,' I reminded him.

'Shay was stupid,' Icepick said.

No arguing with that either. Shay tried to rob a fish and chip shop. Climbed in through a window and fell into the fryer. The Guards caught him covered in grease. They won't let you in to the trial when it's a juvenile, but his brother told me you could still smell it off him when he went into the dock. I said, 'Anybody robs round here is thick. Sure nobody has tuppence.'

'That's why we're not going to rob round here,' Icepick said with a great big lolloping grin.

'So where are we going to rob?' I asked him, trying to sound cool.

Icepick's grin got wider. 'Rathfarnam,' he said. 'We'll do the General's place.'

For a minute I couldn't believe I'd heard him right. The General was your man who walked about the town with one hand over his face. He ran all the organised crime in Dublin – Icepick's brother did a bit of work for him from time to time. He was worth a fortune, but he rented a semi-detached so nobody would know. Didn't work though. Everybody knew where he lived. Everybody knew the place was stuffed with cash. The General didn't trust banks, having robbed most of them at one time or another. But doing the General's place was like signing your own death warrant. Everybody knew that too.

'You're nuts,' I told him. 'Nobody takes money from the General. Unless they want to end up at the bottom of the Liffey.'

'Who's going to suspect two little kids?' Icepick grinned.

It went on like that for a bit, me saying he was loopy, him saying nobody would think of youngsters, nobody would find out, we'd never get caught. I tried to take his mind off it by looking for a Lotto ticket that wasn't past its sell-by, but he kept on and on. Even when I found one it didn't stop him. 'That's an omen,' he said. 'That's what that is.'

'An omen for *what*, ye eejit?!'

The grin never faltered. 'For us making our fortune.'

Sometime between then and the next day I let him get through to me. At least as far as mitching school again and taking the bus to Rathfarnam. That was my twenty pence gone, plus another fifty pence I borrowed from the sister, but Icepick said it was an investment.

Ballsbridge is the poshest part of Dublin, but Rathfarnam's nice. All the same, the estate where the General lived looked a bit run down. Part of the problem was all the battered old cars parked round the place. The funny thing was, they all had their drivers in them, big men with short haircuts, reading newspapers. 'Special Branch,' Icepick nodded. 'The General must be at home.'

'*Special Branch*?' I exploded. 'You want us to rob his place when it's watched by the Special Branch?' I counted hurriedly. There were five unmarked cars and one of them had two men in it.

'They only watch it if the General's in,' Icepick said. 'When he goes out, they follow him. The brother told me.'

You'd have thought he set it up, for at that very minute the front door of the General's house opened and your man himself comes out with the hand over his face. He was older than my da and didn't have much hair, but all the same I wouldn't have wanted to meet him in a dark alley. All the parked cars started up one after another and revved their engines so that half the street was filled with exhaust smoke. The General turns left as if he's heading for Rathfarnam Road and the five cars pull out and start to creep after him in first gear.

'He must know they're there!' I whispered.

Icepick sniffed. 'It's all a game. They want him to know they're following him, and he knows they're following him. They can't get enough evidence to put him in the Joy, but they figure this might keep him out of trouble.'

'How come you know all this?' I asked him, annoyed. But he only gave that stupid grin and tapped his nose.

'Friends in high places,' he said.

He was right about the Special Branch. Every last one of them disappeared after the General. Last seen on Rathfarnam Road like a string of ducks following the mother. He was right about a couple of other things as well. He said there wouldn't be any uniformed Gardai about because there was never any crime in this estate and he said there was nobody in the General's house once he went out. We hung about for nearly two hours and I didn't see a single Guard. I watched the General's windows like a hawk and I'd have sworn the house was deserted.

'It makes sense,' Icepick said as we strolled towards Terenure for want of the bus fare home. 'The General doesn't want any trouble in his back yard so the villains stay away. The Guards know that so they don't waste men on patrols. He won't leave anybody in his house with all that money there because he wouldn't trust them not to thieve it.'

'But leaving money without anybody there is just asking for somebody to break in!' I protested.

'Don't be thick!' Icepick said. 'He's relying on his reputation. Sure, who'd be mad enough to do the General's house?'

I glared at him. 'You said *we* would!'

'That's different,' he said.

I remember my ma did me a fry for tea that night. She must have been in powerful good form for when I asked her for a pound for my bus fare she gave it like a lamb. I suppose she thought I meant my fare to school next day. Anyway, it got Icepick and me back to Rathfarnam. He'd raised a couple of quid as well, so we had the fare back, too. It was going to be some getaway. Icepick was carrying one of those big black rubbish sacks. 'For the money,' he whispered. He must have been expecting a lot. Those things are meant to line a fifteen gallon bin.

The Special Branch bangers were back when we walked into the estate, meaning the General was at home again. 'What do we do now?' I asked in panic.

'We wait,' said Icepick. 'We wait till he goes out. Sure it's not even dark yet.'

'How do you know he'll *go* out?'

'He always goes out at night. He owns a pub,' Icepick said dismissively, as if nobody who owned a pub could keep away from it.

He was right about that as well. When the General's porch light came on and the General walked out, I started to wonder if Icepick had powers. All the Special Branch cars started up and revved then crawled away from the kerb and in five minutes the street was empty.

'Come on!' Icepick started towards the house.

'It isn't dark yet!' I hissed.

'It's dark enough,' said Icepick. Before I could stop him, he was down the side of the General's house heading for the back.

I thought about it for a minute then went after him. I was about as scared as I've ever been in my life, but what could I do? By the time I reached the General's yard, Icepick had the back door open. 'He left a downstairs window off the latch! Can you believe it? A fella like that doesn't deserve to keep his money.'

I could see the General's kitchen through the open door. It wasn't much bigger than our own at home. The sight of it gave me serious cold feet – I don't know why except maybe it brought home that this was real. We were actually about to break into the house of the hardest nut in Dublin and try to steal a bin bag of his money. In fact, Icepick had already broken in, technically speaking. I had the dreadful need of a lavatory.

'Come on,' Icepick said again and disappeared into the gloom.

Oh, Jaysus, should I follow Icepick inside? Or should I just get out before some rozzer turned up and felt my collar? I couldn't make up my mind. If I went in, I could end up in the borstal like Shay Farr, or, worse still, in a box if the General caught up with us. On the other hand, if I turned and walked, I'd have Icepick on my case for the rest of my natural life. He wasn't the General, but he was trouble enough for a fourteen year old.

As against that, if we got away with it, I was out of Ballyfarther. And so was my ma and my sister and even my old fella if he cared. If Icepick was right about the General keeping all his money here and if we could find it and if we could get it back home in one piece, I could take out the grandma and the grandda and all the aunts and uncles and cousins I ever had. It would be like a United Nations refugee mission. But there were an awful lot of *ifs*.

'What are you doing, Durango?' Icepick's voice floated out from somewhere deep inside.

'Nothing!' I hissed, terrified somebody would hear him, terrified somebody would hear me.

'Then get on in here – I've found something!'

That did it. The *ifs* had disappeared. Icepick had found

the money. I was still scared out of my mind, but I headed for that darkened kitchen all the same. As I moved, a heavy hand fell on my shoulder.

I twisted violently, and caught a glimpse of Garda uniform, but he had me firm. 'I wasn't doing nothing, Guard!' I shouted, hoping Icepick would hear. I was dead, but at least one of us might get away.

He heard all right. Half a second later he came out of the back door holding a small box. 'Oh, howya, Willie,' he said brightly. 'I thought I saw you through the window.'

I turned my head and found out what had happened to Willie O'Leary. He'd gone off and joined the Guards. He looked from Icepick to me and back again. 'In the name of God,' he said, 'do you not know who owns this house?'

Icepick blinked. 'No,' he said innocently.

'Only the flaming General!' Guard Willie O'Leary exclaimed. 'You're only trying to thieve the General's house.'

'No!' Icepick exclaimed, eyes wide.

Willie let go of my shoulder. 'Listen, boys, you get yourselves outta here sharpish. I'll lock the back door again and with a bit of luck nobody'll ever find out what you've been up to. You haven't taken anything yet, have you?'

Icepick slipped the box behind his back and said 'No' for the third time that night. Then we both legged it. 'Thanks, Willie,' I called back. I could hardly believe our luck.

As soon as we were well clear, I said to Icepick, 'What did you get? What's in the box?'

He pulled it out from under his coat. 'KFC,' he said.

For a minute I had no idea what he was talking about. 'KFC?' I echoed stupidly.

'Kentucky Fried Chicken,' Icepick said. 'Can you imagine, a fella like the General lives on Kentucky Fried Chicken? There's a couple of bits left.' He offered the box. 'Want one?'

My auld fella came home on leave a few nights later and brought the *Evening Herald* with him. There was nothing much on television so I picked it up while him and ma went off upstairs to catch up on old times. There was a story about Willie O'Leary on page five. He'd been pulled in for breaking and entering and impersonating a Garda officer. The beak remanded him for trial and denied bail. The piece didn't mention whose house he'd been breaking into.

I read the thing through twice, hardly able to believe it. A bit of me even found it funny, although I doubted Icepick would be amused. I glanced at the clock on the mantelpiece and saw it was ten to eight. Ronan Collins would be on in a minute with the Lotto Draw and I still had the ticket I'd found on Monday. But I didn't think I'd hold my breath.

Christmas

John McGahern

As well as a railway ticket they gave me a letter before I left the Home to work for Moran. They warned me to give the letter unopened to Moran, which was why I opened it on the train; it informed him that since I was a ward of state if I caused trouble or ran away he was to contact the guards at once. I tore it up, since it occurred to me that I might well cause trouble or run away, resolving to say I lost it if asked, but he did not ask for any letter.

Moran and his wife treated me well. The food was more solid than at the Home, a roast always on Sundays, and when the weather grew hard they took me to the town and bought me wellingtons and an overcoat and a cap with flaps that came down over the ears. After the day's work when Moran had gone to the pub, I was free to sit at the fire while Mrs

Moran knitted, and listen to the wireless – what I enjoyed most were the plays – and Mrs Moran told me she was knitting a pullover for me for Christmas. Sometimes she asked me about life at the Home and when I'd tell her she'd sigh, 'You must be very glad to be with us instead,' and I would tell her, which was true, that I was. I usually went to bed before Moran came back from the pub, as they often quarrelled then, and I considered I had no place in that part of their lives.

Moran made his living by buying cheap branches or uncommercial timber the sawmills couldn't use and cutting them up to sell as firewood. I delivered the timber with an old jennet Moran had bought from the tinkers. The jennet squealed, a very human squeal, any time a fire of branches was lit, and ran, about the only time he did run, to stand in rigid contentment with his nostrils in the thick of the wood smoke. When Moran was in good humour it amused him greatly to light a fire to see the jennet's excitement at the prospect of smoke.

There was no reason this life shouldn't have gone on for long but for a stupid wish on my part, which set off an even more stupid wish in Mrs Grey, and what happened has struck me ever since as usual when people look to each other for their happiness or whatever it is called. Mrs Grey was Moran's best customer. She'd come from America and built the huge house on top of Mounteagle after her son had been killed in aerial combat over Italy.

The thaw overhead in the bare branches had stopped the evening we filled that load for Mrs Grey. There was no longer the dripping on the dead leaves, the wood clamped in the silence of white frost except for the racket some bird made in the undergrowth. Moran carefully built the last logs above the crates of the cart and I threw him the bag of hay that made the load look bigger than it was. 'Don't forget to call at Murphy's for her paraffin,' he said. 'No, I'll not forget.' 'She's bound to tip you well this Christmas. We could use money for the Christmas.' He'd use it to pour drink down his gullet. 'Must be time to be moving,' I said. 'It'll be night before you're there,' he answered.

The cart rocked over the roots between the trees, cold steel of the bridle ring in the hand close to the rough black lips, steam of the breath wasting on the air to either side. We went across the paddocks to the path round the lake, the wheels cutting two tracks on the white stiff grass, crush of the grass yielding to the iron. I had to open the wooden gate to the pass. The small shod hooves wavered between the two ridges of green inside the wheeltracks on the pass, the old body swaying to each drive of the shafts as the wheels fell from rut to rut.

The lake was frozen over, a mirror fouled by white blotches of the springs, and rose streaks from the sun were impaled on the firs of Oakport across the bay.

The chainsaw started up in the wood again. He'd saw

while there was light. 'No joke to make a living, a drink or two for some relief, all this ballsing. May be better if we stayed in bed, conserve our energy, eat less,' but in spite of all he said he went on buying the branches cheap from McAnnish after the boats had taken the trunks down the river to the mill.

I tied the jennet to the chapel gate and crossed to Murphy's shop.

'I want Mrs Grey's paraffin.'

The shop was full of men. They sat on the counter or on wooden fruit boxes and upturned buckets along the walls. They used to trouble me at first. I supposed it little different from going into a shop in a strange country without its language, but they learned they couldn't take a rise out of me, that was their phrase. They used to lob tomatoes at the back of my head in the hope of some reaction, but they left me mostly alone when they saw none was forthcoming. If I felt anything for them it was a contempt tempered by fear: I was here, and they were there.

'You want her paraffin, do you? I know the paraffin I'd give her if I got your chance,' Joe Murphy said from the centre of the counter where he presided, and a loyal guffaw rose from around the walls.

'Her proper paraffin,' someone shouted, and it drew even more applause, and when it died a voice asked, 'Before you get off the counter, Joe, throw us an orange.'

Joe stretched to the shelf and threw the orange to the man who sat on a bag of Spanish onions. As he stretched forward to catch the fruit the red string bag collapsed and he came heavily down on the onions. 'You want to bruise those onions with your dirty awkward arse. Will you pay for them now, will you?' Joe shouted as he swung his thick legs down from the counter.

'Everybody's out for their onions these days.' The man tried to defend himself with a nervous laugh as he fixed the string bag upright and changed his seat to an orange box.

'You've had your onions: now pay for them.'

'Make him pay for his onions,' they shouted.

'You must give her her paraffin first.' Joe took the tin, and went to the barrel raised on flat blocks in the corner, and turned the copper tap.

'Now give her the proper paraffin. It's Christmas time,' Joe said again as he screwed the cap tight on the tin, the limp black hair falling across the bloated face.

'Her proper paraffin,' the approving cheer followed me out of the door.

'He never moved a muscle. Those homeboys are a bad piece of work,' I heard with much satisfaction as I stowed the tin of paraffin securely among the logs of the cart. Ice over the potholes of the road was catching the first stars. Lights of bicycles – it was a confession night – hesitantly approached out of the night. Though exposed in the full glare of their lamps I was unable to recognise the bicyclists as they pedalled past in dark shapes behind their lamps, and this made raw the fear I'd felt but had held down in the shop. I took a stick and beat the reluctant jennet into pulling the load uphill as fast as he was able.

After I'd stacked the logs in the fuel shed I went and knocked on the back door to see where they wanted me to put the paraffin. Mrs Grey opened the door.

'It's the last load until after Christmas,' I said as I put the tin down.

'I haven't forgotten.' She smiled and held out a pound note.

'I'd rather not take it.' It was there the first mistake was made, playing for higher stakes.

'You must have something. Besides the firewood you've brought us so many messages from the village that we don't know what we'd have done without you.'

'I don't want money.'

'Then what would you like me to give you for Christmas?'

'Whatever you'd prefer to give me.' I thought *prefer* was well put for a homeboy.

'I'll have to give it some thought, then,' she said as I led the jennet out of the yard, delirious with stupid happiness.

'You got the paraffin and logs there without trouble?' Moran beamed when I came in to the smell of hot food.

He'd changed into good clothes and was finishing his meal at the head of the big table in tired contentment.

'There was no trouble,' I answered.

'You've fed and put in the jennet?'

'I gave him crushed oats.'

'I bet you Mrs Grey was pleased.'

'She seemed pleased.'

He'd practically his hand out. 'You got something good out of it, then?'

'No.'

'You mean to say she gave you nothing?'

'Not tonight but maybe she will before Christmas.'

'Maybe she will but she always gave a pound with the last load before,' he said suspiciously. His early contentment was gone.

He took his cap and coat to go for a drink or two for some relief.

'If there's an international crisis in the next few hours you know where I'll be found,' he said to Mrs Moran as he left.

Mrs Grey came Christmas Eve with a large box. She smelled of scent and gin and wore a fur coat. She refused a chair saying she'd to rush, and asked me to untie the red twine and paper.

A toy airplane stood inside the box. It was painted white and blue. The tyres smelled of new rubber.

'Why don't you wind it up?'

I looked up at the idiotically smiling face, the tear-brimmed eyes.

'Wind it up for Mrs Grey,' I heard Moran's voice.

I was able to do nothing. Moran took the toy from my hand and wound it up. A light flashed on and off on the tail and the propellors turned as it raced across the cement.

'It was too much for you to bring,' Moran said in his politic voice.

'I thought it was rather nice when he refused the money. My own poor boy loved nothing better than model airplanes for Christmas.' She was again on the verge of tears.

'We all still feel for that tragedy,' Moran said. 'Thank Mrs Grey for such a lovely present. It's far too good.'

I could no longer hold back rage: 'I think it's useless,' and began to cry.

I have only a vague memory afterwards of the voice of Moran accompanying her to the door with excuses and apologies.

'I should have known better than to trust a homeboy,' Moran said when he came back. 'Not only did you do me out of the pound but you go and insult the woman and her dead son. You're going to make quick time back to where you came from, my tulip.' Moran stirred the airplane with his boot as if he wished to kick it but dared not out of respect for the money it had cost.

'Well, you'll have a good flight in it this Christmas.'

The two-hour bell went for Midnight Mass, and as Moran hurried for the pub to get drinks before Mass, Mrs Moran started to strip the windows of curtains and to set a single candle to burn in each window. Later, as we made our way to the church, candles burned in the windows of all the houses and the church was ablaze with light. I was ashamed of the small old woman, afraid they'd identify me with her as we walked up between the crowded benches to where a steward directed us to a seat in the women's side-altar. In the smell of burning wax and flowers and damp stone, I got out the brown beads and the black prayerbook with the gold cross on the cover they'd given me in the Home and began to prepare for the hours of boredom Midnight Mass meant. It did not turn out that way.

A drunken policeman, Guard Mullins, had slipped past the stewards on guard at the door and into the women's sidechapel. As Mass began he started to tell the schoolteacher's wife how available her arse had been for handling while she'd worked in the bar before assuming the fur coat of respectability, 'And now, O Lordy me, a prize rose garden wouldn't get a luk in edgeways with its grandeur.' The stewards had a hurried consultation whether to eject him or not and decided it'd probably cause less scandal to leave him as he was. He quietened into a drunken stupor until the Monsignor climbed into the pulpit to begin his annual hour of the season of peace and glad tidings. As soon as he began, 'In the name of the Father and of the Son and of the Holy Ghost. This Christmas, my dearly beloved children in Christ, I wish . . .' Mullins woke to applaud with a hearty, 'Hear, hear. I couldn't approve more. You're a man after my own heart. Down with the hypocrites!' The Monsignor looked towards the policeman and then at the stewards, but as he was greeted by another, 'Hear, hear!' he closed his notes and in a voice of acid wished everybody a holy and happy Christmas and climbed angrily from the pulpit to conclude the shortest Midnight Mass the church had ever known. It was not, though, the end of the entertainment. As the communicants came from the rails Mullins singled out the tax collector, who walked down the aisle with closed, bowed head, and hands rigidly joined, to shout, 'There's the biggest hypocrite in the parish,' which delighted almost everybody.

As I went past the lighted candles in the window, I thought of Mullins as my friend and for the first time felt proud to be a ward of state. I avoided Moran and his wife, and from the attic I listened with glee to them criticising Mullins. When the voices died I came quietly down to take a box of matches and the airplane and go to the jennet's stable. I gathered dry straw in a heap, and as I lit it and the smoke rose the jennet gave his human squeal until I untied him and he was able to put his nostrils in the thick of the smoke. By the light of the burning straw I put the blue and white toy against the wall and started to kick. With each kick I gave a new sweetness was injected into my blood. For such a pretty toy it took few kicks to reduce it to shapelessness, and then, in the last flames of the straw, I flattened it on the stable floor, the jennet already nosing me to put more straw on the dying fire.

As I quietened, I was glad that I'd torn up the unopened letter in the train that I was supposed to have given to Moran. I felt a new life had already started to grow out of the ashes, out of the stupidity of human wishes.

Climbing Mountains

David O'Doherty

'Sheep,' said Louis as we set out from the back door of the cottage.

'What?' I didn't understand.

'There are always sheep wandering around on this mountain. I bet one of them has been up to the top.'

'So what?'

'So then it has been climbed before. We won't be the first, like you said at dinner.'

At dinner I had said that maybe in their rush to be the first up the really big mountains – the Everests and the K2s – climbers had forgotten to climb the really small ones.

And this was one of the really, really small ones. Also *climb* was probably too dramatic a word for what we were about to do to it. We were actually just going to walk up to the top of the hill behind my granny's cottage on Achill Island.

'Hang on a second,' I protested. 'Sheep don't count.'

'Why not?' asked Louis.

'Because if sheep count as being the first, then all animals count.'

'So?'

'So if all animals count, that includes tiny microscopic ones. And tiny microscopic animals live everywhere, even at the top of mountains. So then humans are never the first to the top, because tiny microscopic animals have always been there before them.' I spoke fast. I always spoke fast when I was making it up.

'Nothing lives at the top of Mount Everest,' said Louis. 'It's too cold.'

'Not for some tiny microscopic animals. They love the cold.'

Louis marched on ahead, then stopped and spun round to look at me. 'Which tiny microscopic animals?'

I turned to face the sea, and tried to think quickly of a word that sounded like the name of a tiny microscopic animal. 'Eh . . . Alveoli,' I said after a while.

'Stop it with your alveoli. They're something to do with lungs.' Louis could always tell when I was talking rubbish.

'No, it's a scientific term too . . .' Still I tried to keep it going. 'Alveoli are a taytoscopic microbe. They look like little lobsters under the microsco . . .' I couldn't go on anymore. Louis had started to make the low farting sound with his mouth in his elbow that he made whenever our arguments went this way. It always cracked me up laughing.

It was a warm, still, late summer's evening; you only get a couple of them on Achill Island. The sea in Blacksod Bay behind us was flat calm as we climbed over the fence and up on to the mountain. I had a jumper with me, but kept it tied round my waist. Louis was wearing my dad's fishing cap to keep the sun out of his eyes, but soon he wouldn't need it. It was eight o'clock and the sun was sinking into the horizon. Louis reckoned it would take an hour to get to the top and about half that time to come back down again. He knew about things like that. He used to go hill walking with his dad back in Dublin.

Dublin was two hundred kilometres away to the east. Louis and I lived there, about a hundred metres from each other on the same road. We had been staying on Achill with my mum since the start of July. Now it was the end of August and almost time to go back home to school again.

School. I had never liked it very much, but the year just

passed, my second of secondary school, had been really awful.

It wasn't the school part that was the problem; and I had plenty of friends – although Louis and my best friends from round where I lived all went to other schools. But then there were *the lads*.

My school was all boys, with plenty of little groups and gangs of friends, same as there are in any school. The lads were the group in my class who did all the things you weren't supposed to do, like smoking behind the gym, or bunking off to the shopping centre at lunch. They thought they were a bit too cool for the rest of us. It showed in everything they did – in how they would blankly ignore you if you tried to talk to one of them; in how they would all shake their heads and snigger if they overheard you saying something that they thought was stupid to one of your friends. The lads thought everything was stupid. Everything that didn't involve them getting drunk or going to mad parties or doing whatever else they said they did.

The worst part of it was that in a way I believed them. I started to think that a lot of the things I said and did were just stupid. I really tried to change and act more like them – I tried to do what I thought the lads would have done in whatever situation I was in. But that made me feel even worse. I wasn't being me anymore. By the end of the year I was miserable.

Achill had been such a break from that world. There were a million things to do there, things you couldn't do in the city.

Louis and I had built a raft on the secret beach below the house and we could go off sailing on that

or we could play golf on the little golf course covered in sheep

or try to surf on Keel Strand

or fish down on the rocks

or play pool in the pub

or hang out with the local kids

or meet new people at the campsite.

Looking back down the mountain, Granny's and the other cottages were getting smaller and smaller. They seemed to glow bright white in the evening light. Over on the left I could see our neighbour James McHugh walking in from his shed. James could fix anything. Mum would get him over when the heating broke, or when the wind blew slates off the roof.

James had told Louis and me how to make a nightline for catching flatfish one morning as we helped him repair the gutter on the porch. A nightline is a length of heavy fishing line about fifty metres long, with a rock tied to each end. You attach a hook on a short bit of line every three footsteps along it, and then put bait on each of the sixteen or so hooks. Flatfish do most of their feeding at night, so the idea is to bring the nightline down to the beach in the evening when the tide is out as far as it goes, and put it into the shallow water. The rocks hold the line in position during the night as the tide comes in over it. James warned us that we would have to be there early the next morning when the tide went out again, otherwise the seagulls would see any fish we had caught and steal them.

Louis and I made the nightline that afternoon in the garden and took it down to the secret beach at low tide that evening. Standing fifty metres apart, we each carried one of the rocks at either end into the first gentle wave, and lowered the whole thing into the sea. Each hook was baited with a thin sliver of mackerel – the best bait for catching flatfish. We watched as the tide began to come in over the hooks and thought about the box full of flatfish we would be hauling up to the house at low tide the next morning. Louis said we should do it every day. Then we could even sell some of the fish to tourists down at the campsite. I was sure we were going to be rich.

We tried getting to bed early that night. Low tide was at eight the next morning and neither of us was much good at getting up. Louis said goodnight at about eleven. We both slept in the back bedroom. Ten minutes later I followed him in. The light was off and I could hear him snoring gently. I had to feel my way over to my bed. It was windy outside and I was looking forward to bundling up under the covers. I sat down on the bed and felt around for my duvet, but there was no sign of it. I checked on the floor – it wasn't there; on the chair – not there either. I switched on the light but still couldn't see it. It wasn't anywhere. I went out and looked in the kitchen, in the sitting-room, even in the dog's bed. It was a complete mystery. I found some other sheets in the hot cupboard and brought them in, wrapped up and tried to go to sleep. Louis had stopped snoring and was making another noise. It sounded a bit like he was choking, so I switched the light on again. Louis was grand. In fact he was laughing, and pointing at the window. Through a gap in the curtains I could see my duvet hanging outside, blowing in the wind.

Louis thought it was the funniest thing ever. I didn't. The duvet was damp and freezing cold when we took it in. I put it in front of the fire and we stayed up for hours, waiting for it to warm up. I promised to get my revenge.

The wind got worse through the night. A very tired Louis and I made our way down to the beach at eight the next morning to find our plan ruined. There was no sign of the nightline. The storm must have carried it out to sea during the night. We never got round to making another one.

*

The mountain was deceptively high. Each time we thought we saw the top we would run towards it, but then see another top a bit further on.

'What day do you go back to school?' Louis asked as he crossed in front of me. It was so steep now you couldn't walk in a straight line. We were zigzagging from side to side.

'I don't know,' I said. 'I think Mum said something about the third.'

'That's next Tuesday,' said Louis. 'Same day as me.'

It was Wednesday now. Back to school in six days. It felt very strange to be thinking about it again. School hadn't entered my head since we had come down. Every other year I spent most of August complaining about September being so soon. This year the end of the summer had crept up without me noticing it.

'Oh yeah,' said Louis remembering something important, 'I suppose I should say well done on last night with the wheel.'

'Thank you very much.'

The wheel had been the latest instalment in our late night bed-war which Louis had begun by putting my duvet out of the window. A few nights after that I had put a frozen fish in his bed. He responded by putting ice-cubes in my pillow. I got him back by Sellotaping his duvet to his bed another night as he slept. He got me back by Sellotaping my hair to my pillow as I slept. And so it had gone on and on. The night before I had set a beautiful trap to frighten him using an old bike wheel that was lying in the shed. Louis's bed was just under the window and I knew he was a bit scared of the dark. I had tied a piece of fishing line to the wheel and hidden it behind the curtain in front of the window. The line ran round the legs of his bed and over to mine. Just as he was dozing off I suddenly whispered that I had heard a noise outside. He told me to relax and go to sleep. I kept at him and told him I'd heard it again. He told me it was just my imagination, but I could tell from his voice that he was slightly worried. I told him I thought it might be aliens. He told me to shut up. Just then I yanked on the fishing line, the curtains parted and the big old bike wheel landed plonk on the end of his bed. He screamed. I thought it was the funniest thing ever. When he realised what I had done he refused to admit that he had even been slightly scared.

The mountain was much less steep now. In parts it was almost flat. We were getting very close to the top. For the first time the Atlantic Ocean and the other side of Achill came into view in front. You could see the whole outline of the island. Over on the left was the mainland; on the right was Clew Bay with all of its tiny islands. Achill was shaped like an enormous gun, pointing towards America.

Louis let out a shout. 'Here it is!' He was pointing at a mound of stones about three feet high just up ahead.

'What's that?' I was shocked to see anything up there.

'It's the top,' he said.

'But why . . . Who built it?'

'All the people who've been up here before. I've seen these on mountains with my dad. Each person who gets to the top adds another stone to the pile.'

'So we're not the first, then?' I said.

'No way,' said Louis. 'A few sheep, some alveoli and a lot of people have already been up here. There must be a hundred stones in this pile. We are just the latest.'

I looked around and found a rugby ball-shaped stone sticking half out of the ground nearby. Louis had picked up a big flat pebble. We carefully placed them at the top of the mound and sat on either side of it for a rest.

There had been complete silence for a minute when Louis spoke.

'It's crazy,' he said staring out to sea. 'Here we are sitting on top of this mountain, looking around at the ocean and the islands and the beaches, and in exactly one week's time we'll both be sitting in our bedrooms doing quadratic equations or trying to learn off some irregular French verb.'

'That is mad,' I said. I hadn't thought about it like that.

Louis stood up and glanced at his watch. It was just after nine. 'It's going to get dark soon and I want to run down.'

'You go ahead, I'll see you at the cottage.' I preferred to take my time.

'See you in a while then,' he said, jogging off.

I sat still on the mound, thinking about school. About equations and French verbs, about seeing my friends again, about playing soccer at lunch, the teachers I liked, my locker, hanging out after school . . . There was something different about going back this year. I wasn't dreading it at all; in fact, I was quite looking forward to it.

Gradually my mind turned to the lads. They would think my summer had been stupid. What had I been doing? Building rafts and nightlines, and doing mean things to somebody else's duvet. And what had they been doing? Probably going to their parties, and getting drunk and getting off with twelve girls in one night. And they would probably be going on and on, and making in-jokes to each other about it for months. But then it struck me what was different about going back this year. I didn't care what they thought anymore – about my summer, about me, or about anything else.

I knew I'd just had the most fantastic summer of my life. The lads could say it was stupid; they could say and do and think whatever they wanted. But so could I.

For that second I felt like the happiest person alive.

The breeze was getting cooler and the light was fading. I put on my jumper. It was late and I still had to pack my things. I stepped up on to the mound to take one last look at the island and set off back down the mountain towards Granny's cottage.

It was almost dark as I came round the corner towards the front door. Suddenly a bright light caught my eye: a lamp sitting in the middle of the grass. It lit up the whole front of the cottage, and something else beside it . . . something big and bright and pink . . . I recognised it immediately. It was my duvet cover – spread out on my bed – sitting there in the garden. The lamp was the bedside lamp from our room. Louis had even gone to the trouble of plugging it in with the extension cable from the mower. I heard him sniggering behind the bush by the kitchen window.

'Quiet over there, I'm trying to get some rest,' I said, lying down on the bed and pretending to go to sleep.

Flame Angels

Marilyn McLaughlin

Our English teacher, Mr Forester, went all dramatic. It was like a disease. He had a whole new vocabulary. Nobody could understand him. Roxanne said he'd been taken over by aliens. He 'conceived and evolved' a modern, cross-community, open-air version of *Romeo and Juliet*, with singing and dancing to 'point up cultural connections'. We'd be performing on the city walls, over the summer, in good weather if we got any, for the tourists I supposed. That's usually who's on the walls in the summer. Anyway. It's all very symbolic and good for us, he said. He made me go into it because of 'my interpretative skills', and because my 'powerful physical presence' would suit the nurse. Did that mean he thought I was fat? Roxanne said it was because I'm always top of the English class. She was doing Juliet. That's because she's good looking. And he borrowed the boys from the Catholic grammar school. That's what made it cross-community.

We all had our photos in both local papers, the Catholic and the Protestant, posing as if we were in the middle of a scene. Mum was surprised when she saw it. 'A play, Justine? But you're so shy. Still it will be good for you. It will bring you out of yourself. Now where is that mobile? Listen to it beep, beep, beep, drive you batty. How did it get under the sofa? Yes, speaking . . . no problem . . . see you, then. I have to dash. Where's that file? Don't forget about Grandad after school, Justine . . .' Mum had become indispensible since her promotion, always away off somewhere, in a rush.

Roxanne wanted me to go down town after school to meet up with the boys from the play. We were in the toilets, checking ourselves out, in two separate mirrors. I won't be in the same mirror as Roxanne.

'Mercutio will be there, and Tybalt and the Friar and maybe a certain Romeo-o-o,' she said.

'I have to go for Grandad, and Gran needs her messages.'

'Honestly, Justine, I give up on you. I'm doing my best

for you here. You know you like Romeo. I've seen you watching him.'

'Everybody watches him. He's so good.'

'And he watches you.'

'He doesn't.'

'He likes you, Justine.'

I didn't believe it. I'd love to believe it. But I didn't dare let myself. Why would anyone like me? 'And how would you know?'

'All you have to do is talk to him. Then *you'll* know.'

It was all right for her, blonde, skinny, able to walk right up to boys and just start talking to them.

'Come down town with me just for a wee short time and then go to your gran's.'

'No. No way. Anyway, you know I can't talk to boys. I go red. I go stupid.'

The boy playing Romeo was called Eamon. He was a magic actor. He really was. The way he spoke made you listen to every word. You even listened to his silences. And it wasn't just because I liked him. Everybody else thought the same. I heard the teachers talking about him. 'That boy has genuine stage presence. Even when he's doing nothing he makes you watch him.'

'He has a frightening emotional intensity and a visceral power of projection.' That was Mr Forester speaking. When he wasn't being Romeo, Eamon just sat there quietly, with that sad far away look on his face. It was as if he switched off a light. He was quiet, I was quiet. He was no more likely to speak to me than I was to speak to him. I just watched like everyone else.

I liked collecting Grandad and doing Gran's messages. It was better than plodding home to the empty house. Mum's unsocial hours meant that I never knew when I'd see her. Of course I was old enough to look after myself, but it's nicer if somebody else does it. Gran would have a hot cup of tea waiting, and by the time I'd drunk that she'd have Grandad buttoned into his coat and his hat on. She had the notion that Grandad needed frequent exercising, but she couldn't let him out on his own since the time he forgot the way home. She'd hand him over to me, along with a list of shopping and always the exact change.

Grandad was no trouble at all, so long as you linked on to him, to be sure he was always there. The shops were just at the bottom of the hill, along the Strand Road. It all had to be done exactly the way Gran wanted. Peppermints and a bar of chocolate came from the newsagent, along with the local paper, the Protestant one that came out on Wednesdays. It was the only paper she'd read. Bread had to come from the corner shop, along with the baked beans and the bananas. There was a big new Tesco's down the road, but Gran didn't hold with supermarket food.

Just when I'd everything bought, and had plastic bags dangling from every part of me, who did I bump into? Romeo! He stopped to talk!

'Hallo, Justine.'

He knew my name! And before I could stop myself I said, 'Hallo, Eamon,' and then he knew I knew his name.

'See you,' he said and went on by. I spoke to him. I spoke two whole words to him and I didn't go red!

Grandad likes to go home along the quays, as far as the old cattle sheds. We don't tell Gran we go that way. She hates the quays. 'Nasty, lonely, dangerous place. There's always someone drowning in that river. There was that boy only last year – don't know who he was – one of the other sort. You keep away from there.' The cattle sheds are nearly the last of the old quayside buildings still standing. They are big, blind, windowless, painted pale blue, empty. If you bang on the metal doors you hear the echo inside, in the dark where the cattle used to stand waiting. The long blue walls of the sheds cut off the town. In front there is only the narrow concrete wharf, and then the river. I don't come here except with Grandad, but boys come at night, and girls, up to no good. They hang about and lark around. They drink and smoke and write on the blue walls of the sheds. They throw beer cans in the river and leave empty chip bags for the wind to play with.

By the time Grandad and I got to the old sheds there was a light skiff of rain in the air. We stood in for shelter against the blue shed wall. I read the names of all those who come here at night, looking for trouble. But I didn't know any of these names. Then there were the suggestions as to what could be done to the Pope, and travel directions for 'Prods'. 'Go home'. 'Get out'. This is a cross-community wall of words, where both traditions freely express themselves. There was a new one since I was last here. 'Prods start swimming'. I pictured Grandad and Gran and me swimming down the river. Mum would have rung at the last minute to say that she was held up at work and couldn't make the exodus.

I jumped. Grandad spoke. He is not a talkative person.

'What did you say, Grandad?'

'I read in a book . . .' he said.

'Read what in a book?' I asked, because he'd stopped in mid-sentence. He often does that.

'I read in a book,' he said, 'that long ago, before the town was here at all, a man came and saw the spirits of angels burning like flames just above the top of the water. It was Saint Columba, it was. He said that Derry was full from end to end with shining spirits.'

'When did you read this, Grandad?'

'Long ago, in a book somewhere.'

Then he fell silent. We watched the river. There was only water and rain and seagulls, and a smell of seaweed, although the sea is far away.

'Come on away home, Grandad. The rain's easing.'

'That would be a grand sight,' he said. But I didn't know what he was on about.

When I brought him home, I didn't tell Gran that Grandad had been talking. It was so unusual for him to talk about anything that she would have quizzed me for hours. And I was a bit embarrassed for him, because he'd been talking about something so queer. I didn't want anyone to know.

There was a message on our answer machine at home. It was from Roxanne. She'd fixed up a foursome – her, me, the boy she liked who played Tybalt, and Romeo. We were going down town for Italian ice-cream after next week's rehearsal. I rang her at once.

'I'm not going.'

'Oh yes you are, or I'll never speak to you again as long as you live. Eamon's really keen.'

'No!'

'When he heard you'd be there . . .'

'No!'

'Stop with the no, say yes. He likes you.'

So I said yes and hung up. He liked me. I didn't believe it. I'd love to believe it. I would believe it.

The next rehearsal was actually on the city walls, after school. It was an 'acclimatisation' said Mr Forester, so that we could 'internalise our performance space, explore our emotional boundaries and interact with the environment. Stop kicking that Coke can.'

It was a relief to get to the ice-cream shop afterwards. Everyone was in great form, even Eamon was smiling. Tybalt was so funny. He could do Mr Forester's voice exactly.

'Frame the scene, girls, frame the scene.'

Roxanne squawked with laughter. 'Animate your space,' she yelped back.

'Promote the on-flow of emotional unfolding,' Tybalt intoned.

I laughed so much that something terrible happened. I put my elbow in my dish of ice-cream. And then it tipped into my lap and I jumped up and the whole cold mess slid slowly down my skirt to the floor. Everyone in the place was looking at me, and one of the waitresses came with a cloth and a bucket and wiped me down and cleared the floor. My whole head went slowly red. I was sure my ears were on fire, they felt so hot. But the rest of me had frozen into a big solid lump of stupid embarrassment. I felt

Roxanne tugging at my sleeve, to get me to sit down again. Eamon slid his dish of ice-cream into the middle of the table between us.

'Share,' he said. 'There's tons there. You still have your spoon.'

I took a mouthful of ice-cream to please him. But I thought I'd never be able to swallow it. I knew what was going to happen now, now that I'd gone red. Eamon smiled and made jokes but I couldn't think of anything to say. Beside me Tybalt and Roxanne were speaking quietly, just to each other, their heads close together. Opposite me Eamon was beginning to grow quiet and that sad look was coming back to his face. I was trapped in my own silence. The more I tried to think of something interesting and clever, or even just sensible, to say, the harder it got. In the end I gave up. Eamon gave up too. We sat walled in by silence while Roxanne and Tybalt giggled and chattered. I wanted to disappear. I wanted to die. I just can't talk to boys.

Roxanne's dad collected us and gave me a lift home. I ran straight in through the door and straight upstairs. Mum came after me.

'Justine, are you all right?'

'Yes.'

'Did you have a good time?'

'I had a great time. I had a just brilliant time.'

'Well what are you so cross about?'

'Nothing. Nothing at all.' I banged the bedroom door shut and didn't come out all night. I knew that Mum was downstairs on the phone telling her friends how I was so unsociable and difficult. It's a wonder she didn't hang a label round my neck. 'Difficult teenager'. Too right.

The next week crawled by. I didn't want to talk to Roxanne. I didn't want to talk to anybody. I dreaded the next rehearsal. How would I face Eamon? I'd made such a fool of myself. But he wasn't there. Another boy read in for him. He was nowhere near as good. I got hold of Roxanne afterwards.

'Is it my fault Eamon wasn't there? Has he dropped out because of me being so unfriendly? Maybe he thought I was an awful snob and wouldn't speak to him? Is he dropped out completely? I'd feel awful about that.'

'If you'd stop thinking about your own self so much and had had the niceness just to speak to the boy, you'd know why he's not here. And it has nothing to do with you,' she said. She was being sharp with me, but I wouldn't let her just go off and not explain.

'Well what, then?'

'It's the anniversary of his brother's death. He's off school to go to a special Mass.'

'I didn't know.'

'Sure how would you? You never talked to him.'

That afternoon Grandad wanted to go up to the quays again. Away on ahead of us, sitting on one of the bollards behind the cattle sheds was a figure that I knew so well that I could tell who it was even from a distance. It was Eamon – slumped, huddled down into his jacket, staring at the water. I knew every part of him off by heart, just from watching him act. I knew all his moods. It was as if he could speak with his body, with the turn of his head, with the angle of his arm, and I understood his language. I knew he was sad, desperately sad, and far too near the water.

Grandad's very good if you leave him sitting somewhere and tell him to wait. He stays until you go back for him. I parked him on the bench at the end of the Riverside Walk. I gave him the bags of shopping to mind. I knew he wouldn't budge.

Eamon didn't see me until I was beside him. Even then he didn't look at me. There was room on the bollard. I sat down next to him. He didn't move. He didn't speak. I could feel the tiny movements his arm made against mine as he breathed. We both looked out over the river. The tide was very full. You could have leaned down and touched the water if you'd wanted. It streamed past, pulling everything away with it, down to the sea. Twigs, leaves, bits of paper raced by.

'My brother drowned here,' he said at last. 'He fell in one night, just this time last year.'

'Were you here when it happened?'

'No. He was out with his friends, drinking, larking around. I have a picture of him in my head, falling in and being swept away, and I can't get it out.'

'I'm so sorry. I didn't know. None of us knew.'

'Sure how would you know? It's just some stranger in the paper.'

'I should have known. It's so wrong not to know a thing like that. It's so sad for you.' I took his hand. It lay very cold and still in mine. I didn't care whether he wanted me there or not. I didn't try to think what to say to him. It just came. I wanted so much to give it to him, like a present – a different picture of his brother. I told him about Grandad's flame angels, the ones that he said burned on top of the river water.

'Your brother's there with them, I just know it. And he's a flame too. The wind blows them and makes them dance all through each other but it doesn't put them out. Nothing can do that. And you wouldn't know rightly which is your brother's light because of the way they all come together, and flicker one through the other, but he's always there, always himself, making a great gleam over the water. It's just that we don't know how to see it.'

He drew his hand out of mine. I thought for a moment that he wanted to push me away, but he put his arm round my shoulders and squeezed me tight against his warm side. 'I knew you were nice, right from the first time I saw you,' he said. 'I'm glad you spoke to me today.'

I should have been embarrassed, but I wasn't. The words that had come out were so strange and unforeseen that I was beyond embarrassment. I felt very simple and clear in my mind.

'I've to get my grandad,' I said.

Grandad was on the bench, staring out over the water, as if he could see something that wasn't there.

'Maybe he's watching flame angels,' Eamon said, smiling. 'It must be a grand sight.'

I collected Grandad and the shopping. Eamon walked us home. That was a while ago. The play was a great success. Eamon's going to try for drama school. The last time I was up at the quays with Grandad there was a new piece of graffiti on the shed wall – a big heart with my name and Eamon's. He must have put it there.